The Rewilding of Molly McFlynn

The Rewilding
of
Molly
McFlynn

Sue Reed

The Book Guild Ltd

First published in Great Britain in 2023 by
The Book Guild Ltd
Unit E2 Airfield Business Park,
Harrison Road, Market Harborough,
Leicestershire. LE16 7UL
Tel: 0116 2792299
www.bookguild.co.uk
Email: info@bookguild.co.uk
Twitter: @bookguild

Typeset in 11pt Minion Pro

Printed on FSC accredited paper
Printed and bound in the UK by TJ Books LTD, Padstow, Cornwall

ISBN 978 1915853 448

British Library Cataloguing in Publication Data.
A catalogue record for this book is available from the British Library.

To Jane, a true friend

Act One

Hare Moon

One

Leaving Town

We drove out of Newcastle in silence. Enough had been said already. Mam's eyes were swollen, dark circles and she had no makeup on, hair scragged back into a bobble. She looked proper messy. Her roots needed doing. I straightened my hair before we left and had a new nail design. Black and white stripes, Toon colours. I spent ages doing them last night to match my new top. Mam was wearing her usual blue jeans and a pale blue jumper with a small silver cross around her neck. You'd have thought she'd have had enough of blue at work.

I picked up my phone. If I was going to be sent away, then I'd need a way of keeping in touch with my friends. I set up a group chat and added Abby, Shona, Jess, Esmée and Amy. I added Dom too – after all, he was the best dressed out of all of us. Group name: 'The Cutie Cats'. First message:

hi 👋 starting a group chat. being sent away for a few days 😳 not for long. be back before my bday 🎂 can't wait! love u all 🙈 🙊 🙈 xx

I waited a couple of minutes, but no one replied, so I snapped a selfie holding up my black and white nails, touched up my skin, added some sparkles then posted it to my Instagram story. I had two new followers, but they were both suntanned middle-aged men in American military uniforms looking for love and friendship. I blocked them.

A few dogwalkers braved the Town Moor, heads bent against the wind. Rumour had it the Hoppings might not be on this year. Even if they were, I didn't think I'd be allowed to go after Mam found out I got off with the lad that worked on the Waltzer last year, and now this. You could see the cows in the distance across the grass. Weird, that. Cows in the middle of Newcastle.

Abby hates them. She makes us walk miles out of our way, right around the edge rather than crossing the moor using the middle path. Cows are OK if you don't have a dog. We don't have any pets. Nan and Grandad have got a dog, a cat, chickens and bees, if you can count bees and chickens as pets. I couldn't wait to see Meggie, their Border Collie. It's been ages. One consolation, I suppose, for five days of boredom. It was fun going to their house when I was a kid, but we've not been for years and I'm not a kid anymore. I'm not sure why we stopped going. Mam changes the subject when I ask, and she gets angry if I go on, so it's best left. I have kept in touch with my nan –

she sends birthday and Christmas presents and likes me to write her letters. She writes back on a notepaper that smells like the hippie shop in town. I've got all her letters in a box I keep under my bed. Grandad signed his name in birthday and Christmas cards, but I hadn't spoken to him in yonks.

I wanted to stay at home. Shona's mam's a nurse too and she's still going to school. The school is open for key workers. Mam said I couldn't be trusted. After all I've done for her. Can't trust me? Wasn't even my idea. I blame Jess. She always had the ideas but never the guts to go through with them. Can't be trusted? I'm plenty old enough to look after myself. Been doing it for the past two years. Cook the tea, Molly, put the washing on, Molly, run the hoover round, Molly. I've got a life. I've got friends. We had plans.

*

I put in my headphones to drown out Radio 6 and her medley of middle-aged tunes. Mam had that look on her face that said 'do not disturb': lips squeezed together like she had tasted something vile and was trying to swallow. She sat bolt upright, rigid in the car seat, white-knuckled hands clenching the wheel. I was in no mood to talk to her. She didn't ever listen, so what was the point? We got onto the ring road and, ten minutes later, pulled in at Morrisons.

'Are you going to give me a hand?'

'Nah, you're alright, I'll just wait here. Can you get me some Haribo?'

Mam stretched the elastic of a blue face mask behind

her ears, even though no one else in the car park was wearing one, then slammed the car door and I heard her use the f word. *Charming!* I picked up my phone, I knew she'd be ages. Still no replies to the new group chat. I guess it was still early. Anyone sensible was still in bed. I snapped another selfie. I liked my hair like this. It took ages to do, though, and used tonnes of Frizz Ease. The colour was OK, a bit dark, but better than the usual mop of ginger curls. I hate it when they make fun of my hair at school. It is bad enough being ginger: 'mop head', 'ginger pubes', I've heard them all. I get my hair from my dad. It's the Irish in me, he says, that and my green eyes. I have to set the alarm a good hour before I need to go if I'm going to get it straightened for school. I messaged Jess:

morning, wakey wakey rise and shine! ☼

No reply. I tried Abby. She'd be up helping her mam get the newspapers ready in the shop:

hi Abs, how's it going? xx

busy. you?

did you see I set up a group chat? xx

yeah, soz. really busy

being sent to nan and grandad's for a week 😒 xx

bummer! going to town later with Jess 🛍 🍿

😊 well jel 🏠

6

still on for sat? Wagamama? 👫

can't wait. BDAY!!!! Hope you get me something nice 🎁 💎 xx

er, yeah, sure 😳

wanna come to Hype while I get my bellybutton done?

your mam know?

nah, not telling her!! 🙊 she'll never see it anyway. better go can see her coming 👀 xx

see ya xx

Mam's face was tripping her up, so I thought I'd better get out and give her a hand. The trolley was loaded, wine bottles clanking as she struggled across the car park, trying to make it go in a straight line.

'No toilet rolls, no pasta, no tinned tomatoes. It's nuts in there! Everyone's panic-buying.'

'Well, as long as you got crisps and Haribo.'

'Molly, you're not taking this seriously. No crisps and no sweets. You've got at least half a stone to get off. I've got you some satsumas and some Müller Lights to take to Nan's. I know what she's like with all those cakes and puddings.'

I may be fat but at least I'm not drinking myself to death!

*

7

Town, shops and any sign of life were soon behind us. The sky was still heavy, and it looked like it was going to chuck it down. Great! Frizzy hair. We drove along the dual carriageway for miles. I looked down at my phone for a minute, but I've never been good at reading or looking at screens when the car's moving. Past the farm at the roundabout where they have the Halloween Ghost Walk through a corn field. It's *so* scary. Jess's dad took a car full of us last year. They ran off and left me in the middle. I was petrified. A little while later we could see Hexham and the chipboard factory with the chimney that belches smoke into the air. Mam said I used to ask if it was the factory that made the clouds. *Cute, eh?* Past Hexham there were just trees and fields. Trees and fields. More trees, more fields.

My phone pinged as a WhatsApp notification came in. I hoped it was the new group chat I'd started, but it wasn't. Jess had added me to a group chat she had set up. There were loads of people on there, not just close friends. Loads of guys too. I wondered if I should delete The Cutie Cats. No one had commented on it anyway. Was there no point in having two group chats? Everyone was talking about school being shut down and what they were going to do. They were all meeting on the Town Moor tonight.

I sighed out loud and went back to looking out the window.

'What's up?' Mam asked.

'Where do I even begin?'

'Who's that messaging you?'

'Just friends.'

'And what are they saying?'

'They're talking about having a life. You know, meeting

8

up and having fun.'

'Molly, will you stop being so rude. You are only going to Nan's for a couple of days.'

'Five, to be precise.'

'OK, five, but I'm working extra shifts. You're lucky I've been able to take this morning off. The wards are filling up fast. Perhaps you'd like to think of someone other than yourself for a change.'

'Jess's mam says it's just like flu, and everyone is making far too much fuss.'

'Well, it isn't just like flu. This is a deadly virus. People are dying. Molly, I need you to be grown up about this. I'll be back on Saturday, and we'll make your birthday extra special.'

'Are we still going to Wagamama? There are ten of us now.'

'Ten? I thought I'd said six. Oh well, it's OK, I'll phone and ask for a bigger table. I thought we could go shopping together. You can choose your Pandora ring and we can get our acrylics done. You'll have birthday money to spend, and it'll be fun.'

'Mam, this is ridiculous. I'll be fifteen! I was going to go shopping with my friends and hang out at Eldon Gardens.'

'That's what you think. After your performance last weekend, I don't think you'll be going anywhere near Eldon Gardens or that lot. Shoplifting! I'm so ashamed of you.'

'At least I have friends, unlike you.'

'Molly, enough! You were very lucky to get off with a caution.'

I looked down at the new purple Doc Martens I had bought with the money Dad had sent me. They were hurting my feet something rotten. What was it about Docs that made them such torture to wear in?

I shot forwards in my seat as Mam pressed hard on the brake. A pheasant squawked and flapped in front of the car, a mass of bronze feathers, as more of them, each with a personal death wish, strutted towards the car.

'Stupid birds!'

'It's not like they've got decent Wi-Fi. How am I supposed to do my schoolwork?'

'You've only got yourself to blame. If I can't trust you to behave, then you'll have to go and stay with someone who can keep an eye on you. This is not ideal for me either. I've asked a few people and going to your father's is not an option anymore, so I've had to ask your grandparents. This is hard for me too, Molly. If you could stop being so selfish and think of someone other than yourself for once, that would be much appreciated.'

With her rant over, I went back to staring out of the window. I didn't want to look at her. Me, selfish? She could talk!

We turned off the main road, then past ploughed fields and a farm. The road wound through lots of trees, where banks of green leaves, all the same, grew in their shade. It had started to rain and there was a pungent pong of garlic, mingled with farm smells. Why did the countryside always have to stink?

'Oh, the wild garlic's out,' Mam said. 'Your nan makes wild garlic pesto.'

Gross.

*

What with all the bends in the road and the smell of wild garlic, I was feeling car sick so looked up from my phone. The rain was lashing down, water running in rivers down the road. Mam leant even further forwards in her seat, the windscreen wipers going at double speed. There was one last village with ancient houses and an old church. I'd never seen anyone my age there, just old people. The only action it saw was on a Sunday when cars blocked the lanes and people went to church. 'God hour,' Nan called it. Nan and Grandad didn't go to church. Once, I had gone up there on Easter Sunday and nicked all the Creme Eggs that had been hidden in the graveyard for when the children came out of Sunday school. Mam was furious when she found out and made me take them all back and say sorry to the vicar. Nan said Easter was Pagan and the vicar was an arse.

After the village you get to a nature reserve and the big river. I looked out of the window at the green footbridge that goes over the South Tyne to Bardon Mill, the link to civilisation, the train station and the only shop for miles.

Mam was getting annoyed.

'It's like Cruft's dog show.'

She had a point: dogwalkers let their dogs off the lead along here as it's a no through road, and hardly any traffic goes down. They glared at us as we drove along. She wound down the window.

'Can't you put your dog on a lead? This is a road, you know.'

'Calm down, Mam, you're getting road rage.'

When we were little, Dad used to sing 'Time Warp',

and we'd all raise our hands in the air like we were on a rollercoaster as we drove down the last steep hill with Castle Farm in the distance. The farm was an ancient stone building which stood on the top of a small hill and had a square tower that made it look like a castle. Grandad once told me Bishop Ridley who was burnt at the stake had been born there, but I'd never heard of him. The family have farmed there for generations, and they were Nan and Grandad's nearest neighbours. Beyond that was a dead end, dead being the operative word. It was dead old, dead quiet and deadly boring.

Two

Time Warp

Meg rushed out to greet us, barking, tail wagging, a long line of slobber swinging from her mouth. Her coat looked tatty and in need of a good brush.

'Down!' my mother yelled, but it was too late. Meg had left a slimy greeting down her favourite jeans.

The path and steps up to the house were full of plant pots, wind chimes, large chunks of crystal and other random objects. A little stream which Grandad called the burn flowed around the side of the house and at the back was a big garden with a huge greenhouse, Grandad's woodworking workshop, a vegetable patch, and Nan's pride and joy, her herb garden.

Nanny Sarah appeared at the front door, wiping her hands on her pinny, with Grandad Joe towering behind her. She was as short as she was wide, and Grandad was very thin and extra tall.

She'd dyed her hair; it was bright orange and stuck out in tufts from a green scarf that she'd wound around her head. She wore a baggy purple dress under her red spotty pinny and, on her short fat legs, black and white stripy tights. She looked quite mad. I noticed a few whiskers on her chin and an emerging tash. It wasn't a good look.

'Come here, my precious,' Nan said, with her arms stretched wide. Mam took a step back and stared up the lane, arms folded, fingers tapping on her upper arm, her breathing slow and deliberate like she was trying to keep everything under control, but I went to Nan for a hug. She smelt of cooking and incense and was as soft as marshmallows. As I stepped back, I noticed my nan wiping tears from her eyes with the cuff of her sleeve. I guessed she'd missed me more than I realised.

'Oh, you're freezing,' Nan said, rubbing my back, 'you need a jumper!' She held me at arm's length and looked me up and down. 'You've grown so tall! I can't believe you'll be sixteen on Saturday – seems like only yesterday you were in nappies. Oh, nice boots!' she said, looking down. Nan liked anything purple, but, looking up, she screwed up her face and said, 'You've dyed your hair! And what's happened to those lovely curls?'

I ignored that last remark. She could talk, what with her carrot top.

'Well, give her a hug, you frosty old fool!' she said, giving Grandad a poke in the ribs.

I gave Grandad a hug. He patted my back. He smelt musty, of charity shops and bonfires. He wore a green knitted jumper that had seen better days and had food stains down the front. Some of the holes had been sewn up with different colours of wool. His trousers, a mucky brown, were muddy at the knees. He wore a multicoloured knitted hat on his head. Grandad always had a hat on. When he smiled, his face crinkled and cracked, and his blue eyes twinkled.

'How's my girl?'

'I've been better.'

Grandad coughed.

'Still smoking, I see?' my mother said. He cleared his throat then squeezed my shoulder as I edged past him and bent to give Meg some fuss. She'd been singing a song for me.

Mam gave Nan one of those looks that says it all, then one of those hugs that don't mean a thing and kisses that make a sound but don't touch skin.

Grandad stepped to the side to let my mother in. 'How was the drive?' His voice was sharp.

'Fine. The roads are empty. Felt very strange. I think everyone was at Morrisons. It was heaving.'

'Oh, Kate, you look dreadful.'

'Thanks, Mam, you're too kind.'

'Oh, sweetheart, I just mean, well, you look so tired. All those people with this awful virus. It says on the news how bad it is in the hospitals. We've been worried sick about you. We read in the *Guardian* that you don't have enough face masks and protective equipment, and it's only going to get worse.'

'Yes, it's dire, but I'm fine, Mother, don't fuss. However, I do appreciate you having Molly.'

'Nonsense, we're only too glad to have her. It's been far too long, but we don't need to go into that now. Come on in, the kettle's on, and I've made a lemon drizzle cake.'

We stepped over the threshold, Grandad ducking down through the low doorway.

'Have you got mice?' Mam said, her face twisting while she pointed at lots of little bits of black poo that were all over the stone step.

'Pipistrelle bats,' Grandad said, 'we're very lucky to have them. They live up in the porch, see?' Grandad pointed to a small dark hole, right above the front door. 'They eat the midgies.'

Mam and I looked at each other in horror. For once we agreed.

'How old is this house?' I asked Grandad, rubbing my hand on the yellow stone as I stepped through the open door. The walls were about half a metre thick.

'I've heard it dates back to 1555, Molly. It would have been built for farm workers and would have been two houses then.'

I wondered who else had stepped over this doorway and walked into the kitchen, smelling cooking like I could now. I often got this feeling. It happened when we went around castles or old houses. It was as if I could feel the people who went before, as if they brushed against me walking by.

Nan and Grandad's kitchen was the main room downstairs and was warm and smelt of woodsmoke, baking, wet dog and herbs which hung in bunches, suspended on a wooden rack, drying over the Rayburn. A kettle was singing, sending steam into the air. The Rayburn had two big silver lids, which you lifted to put an old-fashioned kettle on the hot plate, and needed wood and coal. It was like Beamish Museum! It sent clouds of smoke into the air when you opened the door. There was a cake on the big wooden table, and plates, cups and saucers that were chipped and didn't match. The chairs around the table were all odd too. Despite all its strangeness, it was good to be back.

The floor was bare stone, and in front of the Rayburn was an old rag rug Grandad had made when I was little. I had helped him, passing little scraps of chopped-up woollen clothes which he poked through an old sack. Proggy matting, Grandad called it. That's how different they were. Anyone else would just go to IKEA. In our new flat in town, everything came from IKEA and matched. Our kitchen was clean, grey and smelt of cleaning fluid. Mam wouldn't tolerate anything out on the worktops. Even the toaster had to be put away.

As Mam looked around the room, I could see her taking in the dust and cobwebs that hung from the beams. There was clutter everywhere. Jars of spices and herbs, books and pictures were piled higgledy-piggledy on the shelves. Goodness knows how Nan found anything in the muddle, but it was homely and colourful, just like her. Mam liked things sterile, too sterile. The shelves themselves were wonky, curved, with carved flowers and patterns. Grandad built everything himself. He was good with wood. He had his workshop outside in a barn where he made wooden bowls, honey dippers, spoons and spatulas, which he sold at craft fairs and at the local farmer's market.

Meg sat down on the mat with a 'humpf'. Susie, their black cat, stayed curled up on Nan's rocking chair. She had opened her eyes as we went in but hadn't budged. I'm more of a dog person. You know where you are with dogs. Nan's chair was in the corner, next to the Rayburn, and there was a big basket on the floor, with her knitting and sewing. There were more bookshelves behind, a small window, and a table which had piles of books, paint brushes in jars, pencils, crayons, paper and paints. To the right was a low wooden door, its frame painted green and shaped like a pointed arch, which led down some steps to Nan's workshop. She saw me looking at her door.

'I'm busier than ever, Molly. I've missed my little helper. I'll be glad of you this week. There is much to be done.'

'Molly has plenty of schoolwork to do, Mother. She's got GCSEs next year so needs to get her head down.'

'I'll get it done, Mam, it's fine.'

'Well then, I guess we'll all be busy,' Nan said. 'I'm on with a new recipe for boosting immunity, and I need to make another load of herbal cough mixture. Every time I bottle a batch it sells out straight away. Your grandad is busy getting the garden ready for the new growing season, aren't you?'

'Aye.'

'Still on with your herbal remedies then, I see?'

'Indeed I am. I'm working on an immunity tonic. You don't hear any of these medics saying anything about boosting our immune systems.'

There was an awkward silence as Nan turned to the stove and Mam looked at Grandad and then out of the window. Nan poured water into a big brown teapot and brought it to the table, popping a knitted tea cosy over the top.

'Now, who's for cake?'

'Not for us,' Mam said before I'd even had time to answer. 'I don't want you feeding Molly with lots of sugar, Mam. You know she has to watch her weight.'

Great. I was starving. I hadn't eaten breakfast, and now here was Mam, jumping in with her diet stick, speaking for me. She often did that, answering questions people asked me before I had the chance to answer as if I didn't have a tongue in my head or couldn't be trusted to give the right answer. She was such a control freak.

Nan raised her eyebrows, giving my mother one of her 'looks' over the top of her glasses.

'There's nowt wrong with the lass, Kate! And there's nowt wrong with having a bit of cake now and again.'

'Yes, well, you and I have very different opinions about food and what's healthy, as we well know.'

Did they have to bicker like this? You'd have thought they would have been pleased to see each other after all this time. Clearly not. Why was Mam always so prickly?

'I'll just have a small piece, please, Nan. It looks delicious.' I couldn't resist some of Nan's cake. She made the best cakes, homemade, light and fluffy. She said it was the eggs that were the secret with their golden yolks from her free-range hens. Mam sometimes got a cake from Tesco on my birthday, but we never baked, not like I used to do with Nan, stood on a chair at the table. 'One, two three, gently all around,' she would say as I folded in the flour. It was only now I was back here, with the smell of baking and one of Nan's cakes to look forward to, that I realised just how much I'd missed her. Not enough to want to stay for a week, though.

'Nothing for me, thank you. I'm due back on the ward this afternoon. Molly should have everything she needs.

She has her laptop and plenty of work to be getting on with. I'll be back for her on Friday.'

It seemed like Mam couldn't wait to get away, get rid of me.

'Now don't you worry about us, we'll be just fine, won't we, Molly?' Nan said, putting her arm around my middle and giving me a squeeze. 'You've got enough to worry about, looking after all those poor souls in hospital. It is good to see you, though, Kate. I'm glad you've asked us to look after Molly.'

'Let's see how this week goes, shall we?' Mam picked up her bag and headed for the front door.

'Have you heard from Daniel, Kate? How's he doing over in Ireland?'

'Don't push it, Mother. Bye, Dad.' Mam looked Grandad in the eye and managed half a smile. Daniel is my dad.

Grandad made a move as if he was going to hug my mam but thought better of it and put his arms down. He swallowed hard, and there was a wobble in his voice. 'Bye, duck, take care.'

As she was leaving, Nan passed my mother a glass bottle of dark red liquid. 'You take good care of yourself, mind. I want you to have a tablespoon of this every day. Echinacea, elecampane and elderberry. I call it The Three Es.'

Three Es? Hilarious. Mam breathed in as if she were about to say something, but thought better of it, put the bottle in her bag and said her goodbyes. The door closed, leaving me with my grandparents.

*

After Mam left, Grandad went out to his workshop, and Nan sat in her chair, picked up some sewing and started humming to herself. I went over to the battered settee, clouds of dust rising in the air as I sat. I looked around, not quite sure what to do, and then picked up my phone.

'What's the Wi-Fi code here?'

'You'll have to ask your grandad. I have no idea.'

'It'll be on the hub, Nan.'

'Again, you'll have to ask your grandad. Don't you have anything on the go, Molly?'

'Like what?'

'Well, any craft projects? Do you still crochet? I taught you how to do granny squares when you were quite little.'

'Yeah, well, I'm not little now.'

'I could show you my embroidery. Look, I'm doing a piece to honour—'

My phone rang. *Saved by the bell.*

'Hi, Jess, two ticks, I'll ring you back, the signal's rubbish.'

I went out into the lane and walked up the hill to the top of the hill by Castle Farm where I could get a better signal and be away from Nan's flapping lugs. I shivered – there was a damp drizzle in the air and I wished I'd brought a coat. There were muddy clarts all over the road and I had to be careful where I trod. I didn't want to ruin my new Docs.

'Hey, how's it going? I saw you'd been sent to your nan's. Bummer, eh?'

'Actually, it's really nice to see her, and Grandad. I

think they've really missed me. But OMG, it's going to be so boring. You remember that school trip to Beamish? It's just like that! It's all home baking and crafting. It's like I've gone back in time. And they still think I'm a kid. Can't wait until the weekend. What are you up to?'

'Not much, just hanging around town with the others. Met Angie Cook outside Maccy D's and you never guess what she said?'

'No, go on.'

'Is it true you went the whole way with Gareth Swindle at Esmée's party?'

'In his dreams. I'll kill him.'

'Wasn't going to say anything but thought you should know Gareth and his mates are saying you're a right slut.'

'Oh, cheers, Jess, just say it how it is, won't you?'

'Oh, come on, babe, you know I'm only looking out for you. It's just, well, the word did get around about you and Davie Thompson.'

'Signal's going, you're breaking up…'

I wasn't going to listen to any more of that. *Bitch!* Gareth swore he wouldn't say anything. We'd both had too much to drink. As for Davie Thompson. Big mistake. Oh God, why did life have to be so complicated? I bet they were having a right laugh, bitching about me. Jess isn't so snowy white herself either. She'd better watch her back. There's plenty I could say about her at the party that night.

It was one of those messy house parties when parents are away that always ends in chaos, something or someone is always broken. You can't not go. That would be social suicide. Emily Sanders' parents were away and so there was a party. I'd gone round to Shona's house to get ready with Jess and Esmée and we'd drank a bottle of Lambrini up in her bedroom. She'd nicked it from her parents' shop. We had a right laugh getting the bus down there. Nearly got kicked off by the driver for smoking on the top deck.

When we got there, it was heaving. Emily's family live in Jesmond, the posh part of town in a huge house that backs on to the Dene. There was a fountain in the front garden, but someone had already been sick in it. I made a B-line for the kitchen to see what booze was there. There was a selection of half-empty bottles obviously stolen from parents' drinks cupboards, plus the usual cheap cider and rank wine. I grabbed some peach schnapps, took a swig from the bottle then felt someone's arm around my waist, their beery breath on my neck. Gareth Swindle. Not the best-looking guy in the world but beggars can't be choosers, and yes, we did end up in a bedroom upstairs. I must have been mad, but Gareth had produced a bottle of Jack Daniel's when we were dancing. I didn't do half the things the gossip-mongers were saying. It's all a bit hazy, but I do remember laying down on the bed, and the room spinning round so much I puked. Gareth called me pathetic and left to join the other lads. I don't remember much after that. Shona and Jess abandoned me as soon as we landed, going off with stuck-up Melissa Baron and her gang, though I did see Jess head off into the snogfest in the garden with one of the lads from the sixth form later on. It was Dom who came looking for me and found me crying in the bedroom. We both needed to get out of there. He'd had the piss ripped out of him for turning up in makeup. Dear Dom, he held my hair as I was sick in more than one rubbish bin on the walk home.

'Argh!' It wasn't fair. Why was my life so crap? I looked down at the purple Docs Dad had bought me; not so shiny anymore. They had mud on them, and probably sheep shit and I'd scuffed the sides. 'Oh, Dad!' I missed him so much: his hugs, his strong arms and solid shoulders. He always knew how to make me laugh, what to do to make it all better. I could do with a Daddy hug right now. 'Oh, Dad! Come home! I need you,' I shouted, and sobbed.

A brown and white cow leaned its head over the stone wall. It looked at me with huge brown eyes and I saw myself reflected in them. As it chewed, strings of slather dripped from its mouth, and its hot, steaming breath hung in the air.

'What are you looking at?'

I felt no better after my phone call with Jess. Worse, in fact. Why did she have to remind me about the party and Gareth Swindle? I was trying to forget it. I was freezing now, my teeth chattering, so I headed back down.

The bank was edged with bushes of yellow flowers, bright against the grey of the stone. I reached out to pick a bit but was jabbed in the hand by sharp thorns. 'Ouch!' But then I reached in, on purpose, pushing my finger against one of the thorns. A bubble of blood appeared. I did it again – the pain felt good. It took the pain from inside and put it somewhere else. The cow that had been watching me over the wall had followed me down the hill and was looking at me again.

'You can sod off too!'

I found an old tissue in my pocket, blew my nose and then wiped my hand clean. There was smoke coming from the chimney and a warm light from the front-room window. I'd have another piece of lemon drizzle cake. I deserved it, after all.

Three

Lockdown

When I got back in, Nan was asleep, head back and mouth open, snoring. The WiFi dipped in and out, and the afternoon dragged. I ate three slices of cake. At least Mam wasn't there to judge. I scrolled through my friends' Instagram stories. Talk about rubbing salt in the wound. The beautiful people were posing, as usual, with perfect makeup, filtered within an inch of their lives. I resorted to looking for cute cats and guinea pigs in hats on TikTok and watched the rain fall like tears down the window. A grandfather clock ticked in the corner.

I must have nodded off but woke with a jump when an old woman with frizzy grey hair and a purple beret walked down the side of the house and tapped on the window, peering in with her face right up to the glass.

'Coo-ee, are you there, Sarah?'

Nan woke too and, yawning, said, 'Ah, Annie, two ticks.'

Nan got up slowly, lifting the cat from her knee, making those noises old people make when they move, then fished in her apron pocket and unlocked the heavy wooden door which led to her workshop with a large black key.

'Molly, be a dear and take the dog for a walk, will you?' With that, Nan went down the steps, shutting the door behind her. I could hear her open the side door and say hello to the old woman.

I picked up Meg's lead from the hook by the front door. 'Come on, Meg!'

We walked up the path to the road and then down the lane towards the green bridge. It had stopped raining, but it was windy and there were deep puddles across the road. I wished I'd borrowed some wellies and a coat. I never wore a coat in town, and no one wore one to school, but it seemed colder, wetter here, somehow, and besides, no one was here to judge.

The lane was deserted. A few sad sheep stood in the field, their coats soggy after all the rain. The dog-walkers had all gone home. I was glad. I didn't want to see or speak to anyone. Meg trotted along, sniffing patches of grass until she chose the best spot to have a wee. That's about as exciting as it got. I could feel my Docs rubbing against the back of my heel but carried on. The wind was shoving me from behind, blowing my hair all over the place. I was glad no one could see me. I must have looked a right sight. I decided to nip to the shop in the village across the footbridge to get stocked up with sweets and crisps. It was a mile there and a mile back, but I needed chocolate. I hated it if I didn't have a stash.

As I walked, my mind flashed back to something that happened when I was ten. Mam and Dad were forever screaming at each other, and I used to go round to the corner shop on my bike to buy sweets and chocolates just to get out of the house. I would buy whole boxes of fudge and scoff them in secret. Mam had been cleaning my room and had gone in my wardrobe. She has a habit of poking her nose into things that are mine. A mountain of sweet wrappers and pop bottles had cascaded out. I don't know why I kept them. Should have just thrown them away. She'd wanted to know where I got the money from and, like the idiot I was, I told her I had been stealing money from her purse. Not much, just the odd fifty pence or pound here and there. She'd been livid: 'Just wait 'til your father gets home.' But he'd sat me down on the bed, put his arm around me and asked me if everything was OK. I wondered what Dad was doing now. I took a selfie with the lane behind and sent it to him: 'Miss you, Dad.' He sent a smile and lots of hearts straight back. 'Good luck! Love you, Molly,' he said.

We got to the green metal footbridge that goes over the Tyne. I walked across it and stood for a while in the middle, remembering when I used to play Poohsticks with Grandad as a kid. The water was flowing fast, and I watched it as it scurried down to Newcastle, past the city and suburbs, and would eventually flow out to sea at Tynemouth. I liked going to Tynemouth. The beach is great. Me and my mates sometimes get the Metro there on a Saturday for fish and chips and a look around the market, then sit on the sand and watch the surfers.

Over the bridge is the tiny station of Bardon Mill. The signs said 'To Newcastle' and 'To Carlisle', but no one was waiting. The wooden gates banged shut as I checked the line and then crossed it. I walked along the platform, careful to breathe through my mouth. You didn't want to breathe in the stink of the sewage works on the other side. As if the smell wasn't bad enough, there were clouds of black bugs as well.

There's only one shop in the village and a pub. Nan and Grandad don't go to the pub. They say it's full of rednecks. I've noticed how folk look at them and talk about them if we go places, muttering 'bloody hippies,' under their breath. The shop was shut. What? I checked my phone. It was only four o'clock. I peered through the door. Darkness. The sign on the door said it was open from 10am–3pm on a Saturday and closed on Sunday. What use was that? I was used to nipping out to the twenty-four-hour garage at the bottom of Chillingham Road or Tesco Express at all hours. I didn't understand how anyone could live out here. It was ridiculous. Dad was right about it being a time warp.

The river was full and flowing fast, and the metal bridge wobbled as I walked back over. You could hear the roar of the water as it surged along. I leant over the railing and watched the churning brown current. I wished it would take me with it. I felt like jumping in. I yelled at the water, 'It's not fair!' Angry tears came. I stood for ages, shouting at the water, kicking and tugging at the metal railing, making the bridge clang and vibrate. It hurt my toe, but I didn't stop. I roared until my throat was sore. When I stopped crying, I blew my nose on a tissue and looked around. I hoped no one had heard me. I was dizzy from watching the swirling water and held on to the railing for support. I thought there was no one around, but as I looked across the surging river to where the trees met the bank, I spotted someone half hidden in the gloom. It looked like a girl. She was only there a couple of seconds and then disappeared back into the darkness of the woods. I was mortified she'd seen and heard me, so I rushed off the bridge, head down, and headed back up the lane.

Meg and I trudged along, me limping with my sore toe and blistered heels, worn out from crying and walking so far. Meg was panting, her tongue lolling from the side of her mouth. She was wet from lying down in puddles and her long coat was filthy, dripping with muddy water. I bet I looked a right sight too. We turned off the lane, and as we walked down the track towards the bridge, I spotted a large brown hare on the path. I stopped, the dog stopped and the hare stopped too. Our eyes met, the hare's big and brown, then it hopped off, under the hedge, and shot across a field.

Grandad opened the door as Meg shook, showering me with muddy water and splattering my leggings. Great! I only had one other pair of leggings to see me through to Friday.

'Hello, you two. Had fun?'

'No, not really. My feet are killing me.'

*

The smell of cooking and the warmth of the kitchen felt good after my cold walk. I took off my Docs, hopped quickly over the stone floor to the rug and warmed myself, leaning back on the rail of the Rayburn.

'We'll have to find you some slippers,' Nan said as she put a dish on the table. A strong smell of garlic filled the room. 'Pasta and pesto, your favourite.'

I did eat pesto, but it came in jars, not stinking of garlic, and certainly not from the roadside, where dogs had weed on it. I managed a couple of bits of pasta, but then pushed the food around my plate, close to tears.

'Put some music on, Joe, it's much too quiet in here.'

Grandad raised his eyes and, leaning on the table with both hands, pushed himself up again with a sigh. He pulled a CD from a rack, opened the box and wiped the CD on the seat of his pants. I could see I'd have to introduce them to Spotify.

'3 Daft Monkeys, OK?'

'Never heard of them, but whatever.'

The sound of a fiddle filled the room. It was better than the awkward silence and me not knowing what to say, or Nan prattling on.

'Do you have to drum on the table like that?' Nan said to Grandad, who was tapping on the table, his fingers spread out in front of him. 'And wash your hands! We have a guest!'

She did have a point: his fingers were filthy, with rinds of dirt underneath his fingernails.

As they ate and I shuffled my food around the plate, Nan nagged Grandad about the noise he made when he ate, and then she quizzed me about school. She said we could do my schoolwork here at the kitchen table in the mornings. She would help me. She used to be a teacher, after all. I wasn't sure what help she would be. She'd worked in a special school with little kids! I guessed Mam had told her about the shoplifting, but I was glad she didn't mention it. It was more a case of Nan talking at me. Grandad didn't say much. He just ate his dinner, which was fine. I didn't feel like talking.

There was rhubarb crumble and custard for pudding. We never had puddings at home. The rhubarb came from Nan and Grandad's garden, but I didn't fancy that either. I don't like rhubarb. Now it was just the two of us, with Mam working odd shifts, we largely lived on ready meals, or I cooked pasta. I could do spaghetti Bolognese and stir fries too. Dad had been the one who really cooked. He made amazing curries, and Friday nights were homemade pizza and sweetie nights. We would have the music on in the kitchen and dance and laugh and muck around while he cooked. But all that stopped when he left two years ago.

I ate the crumble topping and custard, then I looked up at Nan, half expecting her to comment on me not eating the rhubarb, but she was chair-dancing, wobbling in time to the music. I sat back, my head nodding, my leg tapping in time too. It wasn't chart stuff, like I'd listen to with my friends, but it was fun.

Nan had started singing along: '*Perhaps one fine day we can all sail away to a land where money don't count.*'

It was what Mam called 'dum diddley music'.

'Have you seen this band live then?'

'More than you've had hot dinners! We used to go to a little festival as a family in Cumbria, Solfest, and this band played the same stage every year. Your mam and her brothers would go off on their own, with a big group of festival friends, but we'd always meet up when the 3 Daft Monkeys played to check on each other and make sure we were all alright. I think the kids were checking up on us, just as much as we were checking on them.' Nan laughed.

'It must have been brilliant, being taken to festivals as kids. I can't imagine my mam ever doing that now,' I said.

'Did you know, your mam met your dad at a festival? They used to do fire-juggling together.'

'Wow! I can't imagine my mam fire-juggling. She was in a festival band too, wasn't she?'

'Yes, used to give me goosebumps to hear her play. Her saxophone is still up in her room. Shame she doesn't play it anymore.'

'Dad said he'd take me to a Glastonbury one day, but I guess that's never going to happen now.'

'Ee, I remember our first Glastonbury, don't you, Joe? 1984. It cost £16 to get in and we went in our old Morris Minor.'

'Yeah, but we only bought one ticket, remember? You ducked down behind the driver's seat with the sleeping bags on top of you.'

'We'd been to Stonehenge Free Festival the year before,' Nan said. 'It changed my life! I'd had such a strict upbringing. I don't think I was ever the same again.'

'I couldn't be doing with all those crowds, now,' Grandad said. 'We'll stick with our little festivals.'

'Well, maybe we could take you to Knockengorroch next year, Molly. It's a tiny festival, up in Scotland. A proper festival, a gathering of like-minded souls, no commercial rubbish.'

It was kind of cool that they still went to festivals, but I don't think they were the sort of festivals I wanted to go to. Mam said they were full of midges and stinking hippies. My mates and I were planning on going to Latitude next summer. There's a bus that goes from Newcastle. I just had to persuade Mam to let me go.

While Grandad and I were washing up (there was no dishwasher here, of course), Grandad put the radio on. He wanted to catch the news. Putting down the pan scourer and drying his hands, Grandad said, 'Shh!' and went over to turn up the volume. We all listened. It was Boris Johnson, the Prime Minister. We stood in silence as he told us the country was going into lockdown. We were only allowed to leave home for shopping or basic necessities and all other shops would be shut. We were only allowed one form of exercise a day, on our own or with our household, and we were not to meet friends.

If we didn't follow the rules, the police would have powers to enforce and them and fine people.

Nan and Grandad looked at each other.

What did this mean? Would I have to stay here even longer? Would I still be going to Wagamama? What about my birthday?

The landline in the hall rang. Nan went out of the room to talk. I couldn't hear what she was saying, but she sounded serious. It wasn't long before she came back in. She looked at Grandad, then at me.

'That was your mother. She thinks it would be better if you stayed here with us for the next three weeks. She says it's chaos in the hospital, sends her love and says she will ring you as soon as she can.'

'But I can't stay here. I've got plans! What about my friends?'

I got up from the table and heard Grandad say, 'Leave her,' as I ran upstairs and slammed my bedroom door shut.

Four

Friends

Everything felt wrong. I sat on the edge of the bed for ages, looking around the room, thoughts racing. This bedroom used to be my mam's. The walls were dark red, and there was a canvas print from her younger days, taken on stage at a festival, when she played in the band. She had long, bright red hair, a nose piercing and a short, purple strappy dress. Her face was painted white, with a red heart over one eye, like the Queen of Hearts. It was hard to think this was the same person. When did Mam get so boring?

The furniture in the room was all old, some of it painted in random colours. There was a long mirror on the wardrobe door that had black spots around the edge. I looked at my reflection. I looked hideous. My hair was all over the place, my makeup smudged and I looked so fat. I thought of my bedroom at home, with my neat, white dressing table, and all my makeup and products. I fished in my bag for what I'd brought to put on the wooden table and realised I'd left my hair straighteners at home. Great! Frizz bomb hair. I cleaned my face with makeup wipes, found my pyjamas and put them on.

Outside I could hear the roses tapping at the window and the treetops being whipped by the storm. The roof made noises too, as if it were about to be lifted off. There was a howling draught coming under the gap at the bottom of the door. My feet were freezing. Nan was right about the slippers. The room smelt musty, and there was a damp patch in the corner with mould and the paint was flaking off the wall. There were bare boards on the floor and more tatty mats. At home, my bedroom had soft carpet and was decorated in shades of purple. I'd strung fairy lights around my bed. Mam let me choose the colour scheme myself when we moved into the flat in Heaton. It was just the two of us now. Mam and Dad had sold the big house in Jesmond when their divorce came through and Dad moved back to Ireland. It was like someone had put a grenade in our family and blasted it to smithereens. I often wondered what had really happened. Maybe Nan knew? She always had a soft spot for my dad.

I reached for my bag then sat back on my bed. I was glad I'd brought supplies. Despite stuffing down two packets of crisps and demolishing a bag of Haribo I was still hungry. I didn't want to go downstairs, I was embarrassed about storming off, but it was far too early to be going to bed. Grandad had given me the WiFi code, and although it dipped in and out, I spent a couple of hours looking at YouTube, then sent Dom a message. He was my friend from drama club. I'd been going there for years. I loved it.

You could be anything you wanted at drama club. It was OK to be different there.

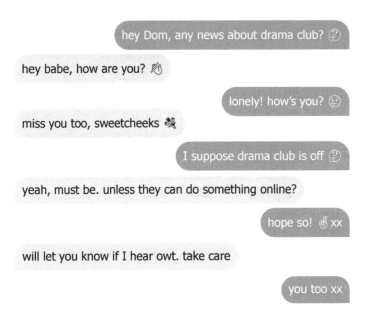

hey Dom, any news about drama club? 🫠

hey babe, how are you? 🖐

lonely! how's you? 🫥

miss you too, sweetcheeks 🥀

I suppose drama club is off 🫠

yeah, must be. unless they can do something online?

hope so! ✌️ xx

will let you know if I hear owt. take care

you too xx

I smiled. Dom was lush. Dom was gay. He wasn't into football or anything the other lads were into. He hung around with us lasses, think he found it safer. We were doing a play in drama club, *The Halcyon Days*. It was inspired by a Greek myth, but Jenny the leader had written it. It was about this couple, Alcyone and Ceyx, who fell in love but angered the gods who killed the guy. Long story short, they end up as kingfishers.

I got sick of the Wi-Fi dipping in and out so stopped scrolling through my phone and got off the bed to look at the books on the shelves to see if there was anything to read. The books that had been my mam's. The covers were dull, mottled with mildew and had yellowing pages: *A Town*

Like Alice, The Hobbit and *Lord of the Rings.* I'd already read *The Hobbit* and thought I might start on *Lord of the Rings* sometime, but it was really long, and I wasn't feeling inspired to read. The film version is brilliant! I wished I'd brought my portable hard drive with films on. There was no way Nan and Grandad's steam-driven internet would cope with a film. I went over to the window. A teddy that had bald patches and only one ear sat looking out of the window. The windowsills were low and wide enough to sit on as the walls of the house were so thick. There were two patchwork cushions on this one. If you sat on the window seat, you could see up the hill to the farm and the tower. Rumour had it the tower was haunted. We'd gone trick and treating up at the farm when I was little, but I'd made them bring me home. We didn't even get as far as the tower after Nan told me it was haunted by a woman in white who sat at the top window.

All of a sudden my phone was going mad with WhatsApp notifications. I opened them up. If they were going to talk about me, then I might as well know what they were saying. As it was, I needn't have worried. I was yesterday's news, and lockdown was what everyone was stressing about.

anyone else's mam losing the plot? 😵 mine's having a right mare 🐗

both mine are up a height. it's the shop stressing them out 🐼

my brothers are a total pain 😼😼 little shits. dad going to have to work from home. house is too small 😵

mine keep banging on about covid, hand sanitiser and masks 😷 got yelled at for selling a woman three packs of bog rolls 🙄

mam has enough bog roll to start her own shop! 🧻 🧻 🧻

I decided to join in with the chat:

at least you're at home! 🏕️ I'm stuck in a field with oldies who eat weeds 🤢 and it's freezing 🥶

well you shouldn't have got caught then should you? 😄 🤷

Ooft! Bang on the nail as ever, Esmée, just say it how it is, why don't you? But she was right, though. If I hadn't got caught for shoplifting, then I wouldn't be here.

*

I had gone down the town as we did every Saturday, wearing a new black hoodie. Well, new to me. I didn't let on that Mam had got it in a charity shop. They were in a big group outside H&M when I met them on Northumberland Street. Esmée saw me coming, said something to them and they all laughed.

When I got there Esmée looked me up and down and said, 'Looks like you could do with some new clothes.'

Bitch!

'Dare you to go and nick something,' Jess said, nudging Esmée.

'Yeah, Molly, dare you to go into H&M and get that

39

top you were looking at last week,' Esmée said, leaning forward, hand on her hip and a smirk on her face.

It's true, I had been looking at a top, but with a birthday coming up I was hoping to get some money. Dad was being generous lately, and although the Docs were an early present, I reckoned I could wriggle a few more things out of him. The others all waited outside, giggling and slurping on McDonald's milkshakes. They thought I'd not have the guts to do it. I'd show them. It was a leopard-print top and was there for the taking. I looked around and stuffed it into my bag then legged it.

The alarm went off, but we ran hell for leather and got round the corner and were almost at the Laing Art Gallery before a security guard caught up with us. The others thought it was hilarious. He knew it was me. I was the only one not laughing. I felt sick.

Mam wasn't laughing either when she came to the police station. She was wearing her nurse's uniform. I was sat on a hard chair across the table from a female police officer in a small grey room, with one window, high up, near the ceiling. There was a box of tissues and a plastic cup of water on the table.

'What the hell has been going on?'

'This young lady has been caught shoplifting. I get the feeling her friends were egging her on,' the policewoman said.

'Is this true, Molly?'

I found I couldn't speak. I wished I could stop crying too.

'*Molly!*' Mam barked. 'You can turn the tap off right now! Was this your idea, or did your friends set you up?'

'No, I mean, yes.'

'I've got no sympathy for your tears. I've had to leave work to sort this mess out. And where are these so-called friends now?'

'Dunno.'

'She's being let off with a caution, Mrs McFlynn, as it's her first time. If it happens again, we will not be as lenient.'

'She's never been in any trouble before.'

'Let's make sure she won't be seeing us again then, eh, Molly?'

'Yes. Sorry.'

The top wouldn't have fitted anyway. It was far too small. Don't know why I picked it. Wishful thinking, I suppose. I'm a size 14 now, but have a cupboard full of 8s, 10s and 12s, waiting until I've lost enough weight to fit into them again. In the meantime, thank God for leggings and baggy tops.

*

I put my phone on silent. I was here for the next three weeks, so I didn't need their exciting lives in town being rubbed in my face. I thought I might as well go to bed, even though it was early, but tossed and turned for ages on the lumpy mattress in the big brass and cast-iron bed, which squeaked every time I moved. It was freezing, despite the patchwork quilt on top. Nan had made it from the old clothes Mam had when she was a kid. Fancy keeping all that, and fancy being bothered to do all that sewing! I could hear the call-and-response snores of my grandparents coming through the wall. The pot of dried lavender Nan had put on my bedside table to help me sleep was not helping at all. It was giving me a headache. Outside something screeched. I checked my phone just in case Mam had messaged. Nope. I thought of Mam, working at the hospital. She was clearly too busy to ring or message me. What if she caught the virus? She was working with all those sick people. Would she be OK? Surely if she caught it, she'd get better? Wouldn't she? I looked at my phone again, pushing the thought out of my head.

Clunk! I heard a noise. Then I heard the squeak of the back door opening and closing. I listened again. I could still hear the odd snort from Grandad, but nothing else. I pushed back the covers, got out of bed and shivered. It was always freezing upstairs away from the warmth of the kitchen. I reached for my dressing gown, the red fluffy one with hearts on that Nan had bought me for Christmas. I used the torch on my phone to see and crept around the bed towards the door. I needed the toilet. The wooden floorboards felt rough under my feet and squeaked as I walked over them. Halfway along the landing I looked out of the window onto the back garden. The rain had stopped, the clouds had cleared and the stars were out. The moon was bright, almost full, and I spotted Nan walking across the garden. She was wearing a long cape with a hood. The moonlight glinted on something silver in the basket she was carrying. After using the bathroom, I looked out of the landing window again on my way back. In the very spot where Nan had been, there was a hare. A big, brown hare, just like the one I'd seen on the lane.

Five

Kingfisher and
Crescent Moon

Daylight was seeping through the thin patchwork curtains when I woke. I couldn't be bothered getting up so rolled over. Dust rose in the morning light, and I sneezed. I felt a familiar cramping in my stomach. That was all I needed. My period had come. I had enough pads for a couple of days, but I was early. I wasn't prepared and I'd need more. Forced out of bed, I sorted myself out then opened the curtains. I sighed. Out of the front window there was a field with dark pine trees at the back, blocking the sun. Nothing moved. No buses, bikes or people going to school and work, no hustle and bustle. No action at all.

I got up and had a shower. The water came out in fits and spurts, and took ages to get warm, but once it was, it felt good. I looked for the shampoo and shower gel but only found little tin pots of homemade stuff: face scrub with oats and lavender and soap with bits in that felt weird and waxy. I dried myself on a scratchy towel, pulled my hair back and tied it with a bobble. On the bed was a handknitted jumper. Nan must have put it there while I was in the shower. You could tell it was one of her creations – they had a 'style' that was all their own. This one was made with lots of little stripes of different colours using odds and ends of wool. I put it on over a pair of clean leggings and looked in the mirror. You could have fitted two of me in it. The sleeves came down to my knees. I laughed out loud, took a photo and snapped it to Jess for a laugh:

> don't show this to anyone but look what my nan has given me 😄 pmsl 😄

Nan was in the kitchen. She was wafting a bunch of burning leaves around and muttering to herself. It stank.

'Thanks for the jumper, Nan.'

'Oh, you made me jump! I thought you could do with it, what with those thin tops you wear. I made it for your mam when she was your age.'

'What are you doing?'

'Smudging. Sage is used for getting rid of negative energy.'

'Negative energy?'

'Oh, you know, bad feeling, resentment, regrets. Your mother left quite a trail behind her. Then there's Boris Johnson and his disgrace of a government.'

I didn't know what to say. I always knew Nan was a bit odd, but she seemed to be getting madder. As for regrets and resentment – there was clearly something I didn't know, but now was not the time to ask.

She looked at me over the top of her red-framed glasses. 'You look like you could do with a hug.'

I melted into her arms and let myself be hugged. 'I've got my period. It came early, I feel rubbish. Have you got any paracetamol?'

'What you need is a nice cup of mugwort tea. Just the job for your monthlies. We'll both have some. It's good for us menopausal women too. Might add some sage to mine, these hot flushes are driving me nuts! Covers on, covers off. Drives your grandad mad with all my sweating and fidgeting at night.'

'I saw you out in the garden last night. What were you doing? Were you trying to cool off?' I laughed.

Nan looked at me, hesitated for a moment, then said, 'I was picking herbs, Molly. Some are better gathered under the powerful energy of the moon. I got a big basket of mugwort. It looks quite magical with the moonlight reflecting off its silver leaves.'

I wasn't expecting that for an answer. It didn't explain the hare, either.

I took a couple of sips of my tea, but it tasted bitter. I managed to tip the rest down the sink when Nan wasn't looking. She was back to her smudging and muttering. I left her to her wafting and went outside to see what Grandad was up to. He was in his veggie patch, digging. A blackbird was hopping on the ground beside him.

'She's looking for worms,' Grandad said, as he saw me watching over the fence. 'Nice jumper,' he added with a smile and a wink.

'I look ridiculous.'

'Have you had breakfast, Molly?'

'No, not yet. Nan was too busy stinking the house out, so I left her to it. Can I just have a piece of toast, please, Grandad? I feel a bit sick.'

'You sit here, and I'll bring us a nice cup of tea and a slice of toast and honey, and after that, we'll walk down to the nature reserve.'

I sat down, listening to the water tumbling over the rocks. Grandad had made a wooden bench by the burn, with a sun carved into the back – 'the sunny seat', Nan called it – and they would sit there and watch the sun go down together. They were dead romantic at times, those two. There was a rope swing hanging from the branches of the sycamore tree, and I thought of all the summers when I would come and play in the stream, building dams and making rock stacks. When it had been raining hard, the river would rise and become dangerous. It rose quickly, changing from a clear, trickling stream to a raging brown torrent, and I was always told to keep away when the river was 'in spate', as Grandad called it.

Grandad came with the tea and toast and sat down next to me on the bench. He pointed to the water downstream, where a pair of ducks were inspecting the riverbank. One was brown, but the other had a bright green head with a yellow beak and a white stripe around its neck.

'They come here every year to the same spot, to lay their eggs in a nest on the bank. They're mallards.'

They started quacking and it sounded like they were laughing.

'They are kind of cute. I wonder if they'll have baby ducks?'

'Ducklings,' Grandad said.

'Yeah, I know,' I said, raising my eyes and smiling.

'I'm done with my digging, fancy a walk?'

At the mention of the word 'walk', Meg jumped up and started barking.

'Yeah, why not. There's not much else to do.'

*

The first of the new-born lambs were bouncing around the fields, tails bobbing, making high-pitched bleating sounds. As we walked, sheep called their young with deep-throated baas and the little ones scampered to them, biffing their mothers' udders, which were swollen with milk.

'Why do they have elastic bands on their tails?'

'It's so the tails drop off,' he said. 'It's to prevent them getting blowfly.'

'Doesn't it hurt them?'

'No, and besides, you don't want blowfly laying their eggs in the skin. Short tails keep the dags down so flies aren't attracted to the warmth and moisture.'

'Dags?'

'Poo.'

I screwed up my face. 'I could never be a farmer.'

Grandad laughed. 'That's nothing, just you wait until they castrate the males.'

'Eugh! Enough.'

We carried on walking down the lane; the roadside

hedges had bursts of tiny white flowers. I hadn't noticed them yesterday.

Grandad saw me looking at them. 'The blackthorn is in bud, the seasons march on, Molly.'

'It's really pretty, but why isn't it all in flower?'

'That's because it's a mix of hawthorn and blackthorn.'

'How can you tell which is which?'

'Blackthorn gets the flowers before the leaves, and the hawthorn gets its leaves before the flowers.'

Once you got Grandad talking about something he was interested in, he had plenty to say. It was nice, being with him like this. I could see he was enjoying it too.

'I make sloe gin for Christmas from the blackthorn, and your nan uses the hawthorn in her remedies. Do you remember your first taste of a sloe berry, Molly? Your face was a picture!'

'Ha! I'll never forget, and I'll not fall for that one again. It felt like my mouth was being turned inside out. It was revolting. I'll pick some for Nan.'

'Oh no, Molly, leave it where it is. They say it's unlucky to bring the blossom of the blackthorn into the house. If we find any decent branches, though, I might just gather a bit on our way back. I've sold three walking sticks this past month at the farmers' market. I've got my gloves in my pocket. Spiny little devils, they are.'

I thought of the thorns I'd dug into my thumb on the first day I was here and buried my hands deep into my pockets.

We walked on, down the lane and past the green bridge. It was no use going to the shop today, it was Sunday. I could hear the church bell ringing up in the village. A solitary bell that clanged. It didn't sound very inviting.

We entered the nature reserve by the bottom path, walking along the sandy bank. Mam and Nan used to bring us down here, with picnics and buckets and spades in the summer holidays here when I was little. I could hear my mam's laugh as she rolled up her trousers and paddled in the cold water. The water was still high in the river, flowing fast, too fast for paddling. Along the bankside there were big pink knobbly buds pushing through the sand.

'Butterbur,' Grandad said after he saw me looking at them. 'In the olden days, they used to wrap butter in the leaves to keep it cool. It was used in the plague times to reduce fever, and your nan still uses it to treat migraines.'

Who needed Google when you had my grandad? I wondered about Nan and all these flowers and leaves she was using, her midnight moonlit wanderings, her locked room and the old hag who had visited her. Was she some sort of witch?

We walked further along, through the trees, where roots made the path bumpy and pine branches touched like turnstiles to another world. Away from the roar of the river, it was silent, dark, with overgrown bushes, fallen-down trees covered with ivy that we ducked under and climbed over. We went deeper into the woods, past the point where the river splits and flows around a small island.

We once camped out on the island, Grandad, and me. We collected wood, lit a fire and stuck marshmallows on sticks to toast. There were stones you could stand on, but with all the rainfall, the river was swollen, and they were hidden under the water. Meg had found a stick and was wanting me to throw it. She swam out to it, then brought

49

it back, shaking river water all over me and barking for me to throw it again.

Grandad and I sat for a while on a fallen tree trunk, which was worn smooth on top from where people had sat on it before. Grandad rolled a ciggie. I could have murdered one, not that I was into rollies, but it would have been better than nothing. I breathed in his smoke instead. We didn't speak. I watched the water, imagining it flowing all the way back to Newcastle. A flash of bright blue shot by.

'Did you see that?'

'That was a kingfisher,' Grandad said. 'You don't often see them, but when you do, they are a very special thing. Folk reckon the kingfisher is the bringer of good weather and good fortune. Let's hope so.'

'I could do with some good luck, Grandad!'

As I listened to the gurgling stream, I thought about Mam. What if she got Covid? She was always looking after other people. Who would look after her?

Grandad Joe reached out his arm and squeezed my leg, as if he knew what I was thinking about. 'It'll all be alright, just you see,' he said.

Tears pricked in my eyes. As I turned away, looking down, I caught sight of something. On the ground in the mud was a small, green stone. I picked it up and saw it was a crescent moon. It had two tiny holes at the tips at either end and was threaded in the middle of a length of red string.

'What's that you've found?'

'I'm not sure.'

'Let me see. Red thread, eh? The moon is made from malachite. Your nan will be very interested in this, I dare say. It looks old. Come on, let's get back and show her. Must be time for lunch.'

'Can you tie it around my wrist?'

Grandad looped the red thread around my wrist then tied a knot. I turned my hand over and looked at the little green moon. I wondered who had dropped it. It reminded me of the friendship bracelets we used to make in junior school. As we stood up to go, we both smelt smoke at the same time. Looking across to the island, there was a thin white coil rising into the air.

'Well I never, someone's over there,' Grandad said.

Six

Spinach Pie

I burst through the back door. 'Grandad took me to the nature reserve. We saw a kingfisher. It was bright blue, and I found this, look!'

Nan was in the kitchen, laying the table for lunch. 'Let me see.'

I showed her the red string bracelet with the green crescent moon.

'Well, I'll be blowed,' Nan said, holding my wrist in her hand. 'It's a charm bracelet, an amulet. The moon is made from malachite, the stone of transformation and protection. It looks old. Where did you find it?'

'I found it on the ground, next to the tree trunk seat, just after the kingfisher had flown by. Then we saw smoke, we think someone might be camped over on the island.'

It was soup for lunch, and Grandad's homemade bread. *Here we go again.* I'd got carried away with the kingfisher and the little moon bracelet but was brought back down to earth with a bang. The soup was a dull green with bits of darker green floating in it, and the bread was as hard as the stones that built the walls down the lane. Who in their right mind eats green soup? What I would have given for tin of tomato soup and a packet of white sliced! I put the tiniest amount on the tip of my spoon and, careful not to inhale at the same time, put it to my lips.

'Molly, just eat your soup, it's made with the new season's nettle tips, full of iron and vitamins,' Nan said. 'Just what you need at your time of the month.'

'Nan, really! I have tried it, it's minging!'

'Molly! Don't speak to your nan like that,' Grandad said. 'You've hardly eaten anything since you came. This is good, wholesome food. You'll waste away.'

Here we go again. Battles over food.

'Can we not have some proper food, instead of all these weeds and green things? Soup comes in tins, and I like sliced white bread.'

'You know fine well we believe in eating simply, growing what we can and not destroying the planet by importing food from halfway around the world, wrapped in plastic,' Grandad said. 'We eat with the seasons, and nettle tops are a wonderful source of food this time of year. Just eat it.'

I picked up a chunk of bread and dipped a corner in the soup. I gagged. 'I'm sorry, I can't eat this.'

My eyes filled with tears as I pushed my bowl away, and once I'd started crying, I couldn't stop. I went over to the sink and pretended to be washing up, the tears falling silently into the bowl. Nan and Grandad ate their lunch in silence, and I wished the ground would open and swallow me up. I'd upset them, I knew, but I was upset too.

*

After lunch, Grandad went back out to the garden, and Nan went into her workshop. I used to love helping her in there when I was little. I think it was because I could have her all to myself. I was her precious, and she would lift me up on to one of her stools and tell me the names of the plants and flowers she used. She showed me how to draw them, and then we would draw together, she in a big leather-bound book, me in a little wire-bound notebook with a spotty cover that I took along every time I went to her house. I've still got it somewhere at home and I think it's because of her spending all that time teaching me to draw that I'm doing art GCSE. I want to go on to do art and drama A-Level, but Mam wants me to do science. Biology's not that bad, but I hate physics.

'Can I help?' I asked, standing on the top step of the workshop, my voice timid and quiet.

'Come on in, Molly. This isn't easy, is it? It's been so long since we've seen you and I guess we're out of touch with the ways of trendy young people, living here in our bubble down the lane.'

Not easy? She could say that again. Nothing made sense anymore. I went down the three stone steps into Nan's workshop. I felt awkward, didn't know where to stand or sit. I went over to a shelf and looked at her rocks and crystals while I spoke.

'It's certainly very different to town life. I always knew that, but when I was a kid, it was fun, like an adventure. We came for holidays and sleepovers, and then all that stopped. What happened? Why did we stop coming?' I turned to face Nan.

'We were so upset at their divorce. I always had a huge soft spot for your dad. But I think that's a conversation for you and your mam to have. I don't feel it's my place to tell you everything, and there are always two sides to every story.'

'But why did she stop me seeing you?'

'Oh, maybe I poked my nose in where it wasn't welcome, said too much. I can speak before I've engaged my brain sometimes. We thought we'd lost you, Molly. Now you're here, I don't want to lose you again. Your grandad took it very hard.'

'I don't think Mam cares about anything but her work.'

Nan sighed and moved in closer. 'Oh, Molly, these are difficult times. The pandemic is filling up the hospitals, and you know your mam will be in touch just as soon as she is able. Now, my darling, let's see what we can do for your tummy. Still sore? Your mother used to get such heavy periods.'

Nan reached up to the shelf and got down a big jar, full of dried leaves and petals. It said 'Monthly Moon Time Blend' on the label.

'There's many a woman who swears by this. It was my grandmother's recipe, see?'

Nan turned the pages in her big leather book, and in faded ink, with beautiful lettering, there was the recipe for Monthly Moon Time Blend.

There were shelves on two sides of the room, with jam jars labelled in Nan's flowery writing, and drying racks, where plants and flowers were laid out on trays. While Nan went into the kitchen to boil the kettle, I looked along her workbench. There was a large pestle and mortar, her big leather-bound book which she wrote everything down in, illustrated with little drawings of leaves and flowers, smaller notebooks, and trays that held brown paper packages, labelled according to what was in them. In the corner was a locked cupboard and in there plants that Nan said had to be used very carefully and only by those with the 'knowledge'. Her treatment bed on which she gave crystal healings and massages was along another wall, with shelves of crystals above it. Under the window, which looked out onto the back garden, two armchairs sat side by side, with a coffee table in between. There was a box of tissues on it, and a vase of daffodils. I sat down in one of the chairs and looked down the garden at the borders where Nan grew her herbs. Plants of different shapes and sizes, that looked cared for and loved.

Nan came back with a red spotty teapot and two slices of homemade gingerbread. Then she held my hand and looked again at the little green moon.

'I wonder who it belonged to? They may well be missing it.'

'Grandad thought there may be someone camped over on the island.'

'Strange to think of someone camping during a lockdown. But some to think of it, there was a homeless guy there last winter, sleeping in a little blue tent. I was so worried about him. I wondered at the time if he was one

56

of those refugees. There were complaints about human excrement in the woods. The parish council and that brute of a man from the farm by the bridge got him chased off. I often wonder what happened to him.'

'Now, enough chatter. We need to get to work. This Covid business is nasty, and the medics don't yet know how to treat it. I want to make some immune-strengthening tonic, and some more of my sore throat gargle and cough mixture.'

We spent a couple of hours mixing and blending the different herbs and potions from Nan's shelves. All the time, she was telling me about what they were for: echinacea root, elderberries and elecampane root for boosting the immune system. Things with funny names that I'd never heard of, but Nan said she gathered them in the woods: turkey tail fungus, birch polypore. It was so interesting. I wondered why all this herbal medicine was just a hippie thing.

We were bottling the last of some elderberry tonic when there was a knock at the side door. It was a stable door, and Nan opened the top half.

'Ooh, Effie, how lovely to see you. How can I help?' Nan said.

'Is it OK to come in, Sarah? I've got a mask.'

'Oh, good heavens, no need for that, Effie!' Nan said.

'Are you sure? Perhaps we'd better leave the door open for some fresh air, then.'

The lady, Effie, looked flustered and as if she were on the verge of tears, so I excused myself and went up to my bedroom. I pulled my laptop out of my school bag and logged on to Google Classroom. This was where we shared any work we'd done. I had plenty to do, but not much of it inspired me. There were emails from our form teacher, saying it was up to us to find our own rhythm with work and asking if we had any problems. Ha! Where do I even begin? I closed the laptop and went over to the window seat.

The tall trees opposite were swaying in the breeze, their tops waving, the clouds hurrying past. I saw Effie leaving, walking through the garden, and so went back down to Nan. She was in her rocking chair, her needlework on her lap.

'Is your friend OK?' I asked Nan.

'Sort of. I was able to give her something for her nerves. She's terrified of this virus, and unlike you, her grandchildren are not allowed to visit her. She's missing them dreadfully.'

'What are you making, Nan?'

'It's some embroidery on a piece of fabric I've been sent as part of a project called the Silver Spoon Collective.'

Nan spread a small piece of fabric out on her knee. There was a spoon shape printed on it, which Nan had gone around with red thread in chain stitch, and she'd started to embroider some flowers on it.

'What's the Silver Spoon Collective?'

'It's a project to bring women together to honour the women murdered on charges of witchcraft. You send off for a name then make a sampler that will be hung alongside all the other names as part of an exhibition. A bit like prayer flags.'

'We've been learning a bit about the burning times in history.'

'They were terrible times and thousands of women were murdered for being witches, not just here but all over the world, often for nothing more than being poor and on the margins of society. It didn't pay to stand out from the crowd or upset your neighbour.'

'What name have you been given?'

'I've been given the name of Ann Watson. I don't know much, other than she was one of fifteen women, hanged on the Town Moor in Newcastle in 1650.'

'The Town Moor, where the Hoppings are held?'

'The very same.'

'I'm going to embroider Ann's name in red thread, and maybe do some flowers around the edge, and maybe some blue swirls to represent the Tyne and Newcastle.'

'What had Ann done?'

'I've no idea. Her name is from a list of those hanged, but I don't know anything else. I do know these women would most probably have been tortured until they confessed to having pacts with the Devil, but I don't know any specific details. I've been meaning to do some more research. Maybe you could help, Molly; you're good with the internet.'

We sat by the Rayburn, and as Nan did her sewing I checked my phone. No messages, and nothing that really grabbed my attention. I picked up a book about herbal remedies and started leafing through it. I was interested in the drawings. I thought I might like to do some of my own.

Around five o'clock, my phone rang – it was Mam.

'Hi, Molly, how's it going?'

'It's OK, I'm helping Nan in her workshop. We're making loads of remedies to help people with Covid.'

'Oh yes, I was worried my mother might be trying to rope you into her ways.'

'I don't mind, Mam, and anyway, it's interesting. There's not much else to do.'

'You've got schoolwork to do! Plenty of it too, I shouldn't doubt.'

'It's Sunday. I'll start tomorrow.'

'I don't want you getting behind, Molly. What about food? You did so well with the Slimming World plan last month. You don't want to put that half stone back on again. I hope you're sticking to three Syns a day.'

'It's not great. It's impossible to follow the plan and stay on track. I know I shouldn't be eating cake but I'm starving. They eat weeds, as you well know. Everything comes from the garden. I could murder a pizza! And I've started my period.'

'Molly, just do your best. It's only for three weeks. I'll have to go, speak soon. Love you.' She rang off.

I sat with my phone in my hands looking at the blank screen. So that was it. Schoolwork and dieting. I didn't get the chance to say much else. She was so prickly, always in such a rush these days. She never had any time for me. We never sat down and talked, did anything together, like I'd done with Nan in the workshop this afternoon.

'How's your mother?' Nan asked. 'Did you wish her a happy Mother's Day?'

*

It was getting dark by the time we stopped working and went into the kitchen to find Grandad. He'd been busy and was taking a pie out of the Rayburn as we went in. It smelt wonderful and I was starving. We never had pies at home, all that pastry! Thank goodness for Greggs. I passed one on the walk home from school. Steak bakes were my absolute favourites, with cheese and onion slices coming a close second.

'Mmm, looks great, Grandad.'

'Yep. Jolly glad I planted this spinach in the greenhouse in the back end. It's a lean time of year this, after the winter.'

'Spinach, in a pie?' My heart sank.

I tried to eat it. I really did. It was the texture. All slimy, with bits of grit in. Hot tears fell down my cheeks.

'What's up, duck?' Grandad said, his voice kind, which just made it worse.

'I'm just not used to all of this,' I said, waving my hand around, snot bubbling from my nose. It wasn't just the food. I missed my friends – none of them had been in touch. I missed my mam, even though she nagged, and I felt terrible for not asking how she was and not remembering it was Mother's Day. It was no surprise I had a headache. Grandad looked nervous, like he didn't know what to do or say, then looked to Nan, who was reaching for a box of tissues.

She came up behind me and folded her arms around my chest, leaning her head on my shoulder. She spoke gently into my ear. 'We love you, Molly, don't cry. Tell us what we can do to help. We want you to be happy here. What is it you need?'

I brushed her off and stood up. 'I'm sorry, I need food I can eat – you know, chips, pizza, pasta and not with all this green stuff!' I pointed at the spinach pie on my plate.

Green water was oozing from the pie. 'I need to go to the shops. There are other things I need too. I think I'll just go to bed if that's OK?'

'Alright, off you go, but I'll come up in a bit with some supper for you,' Nan said, 'something I know you'll like.' Nan smiled, letting me go.

I lay down on the bed and sobbed. My whole world was turned upside down. Nothing made sense anymore. The news was just awful: hundreds of people dying from Covid. They'd even showed the bodies piled high in the morgue on the news. I was scared and lonely. I wondered about phoning Dad but didn't want to bother him. I wondered about ringing Jess but just wasn't sure. She hadn't got back after I'd sent her the picture of me in my jumper, and I couldn't be bothered with the group chat. I knew who I'd talk to: Dom. I tried his number, but he didn't pick up. I left a message.

Just then, there was a knock on the door. Nan appeared with her wooden tray and on it, a pretty cloth, a little vase of flowers and a bacon sandwich, oozing with ketchup.

'Thought you could do with a bacon sarnie. David from up at the farm has just sent down a load of bacon and sausages. Gloucester Old Spot, free-range pigs.'

I laughed. Typical! Our bacon came from Tesco!

'There. That's better, nice to see a smile. Grandad and I have been talking. There are a few things we need, so how about a trip to Hexham tomorrow? Someone's got a birthday coming up next week, after all.'

'Thanks, Nan, you're the best.'

'Oh, my precious girl. Try the tea, it's lemon balm. It'll help soothe you.' Nan held my head gently in her hands and gave me a soft kiss on the forehead. 'We love you, Poppet.'

'I love you too, Nan,' I whispered, tears flowing once again.

Seven

The Girl

I'd slept well, a deep sleep, dreaming about swirling rivers, green moons and a woman with long silver hair who'd held out her hand and pulled me from the water. As I laid in bed, I listened to a bird outside. It was making one heck of a racket. The smell of bacon cooking reached my nose, and I got up, hungry for breakfast. Grandad was downstairs, cooking.

'How about a Daddy breakfast?'

A 'Daddy breakfast' was a big fry-up and harked back to the days when my mam and her brothers were kids and Grandad cooked everyone's breakfast on a Sunday – the full works: sausage, bacon, eggs, beans, tomatoes and mushrooms.

The sausages were delicious, as was the bacon. As well as forever dieting, Mam had gone vegan after watching a

64

documentary about the meat industry, so I hardly ever had meat these days.

'I'm surprised at you and Grandad, eating meat. I thought it was really bad for the planet. Lots of my friends are vegans.'

'Well, for starters, the meat we get is locally produced, free-range and grass-fed, or as with the pigs this bacon came from, they root around in the trees, having a good life. The guy we get our beef from sings to his cows. He plays his flute to them.'

'It tastes loads better too,' I said, spearing a fat sausage.

'It's expensive, mind you, and it isn't a total solution to the problem. If all meat were farmed this way, we would need a lot more room for the animals, which leads to more over-grazed land and less biodiversity. You see, it's complicated. We should all eat a lot less meat.'

'No McDonald's then?'

'Definitely no McDonald's!'

'Do you eat your chickens?'

'Yes, of course we do! If there are surplus cockerels, then they go in the pot,' Grandad said, 'though that's my job, your nan is far too soft to wring a chicken's neck.'

Nan was sitting with a pad of paper making a shopping list.

'Righteo, birthday girl, anything you fancy?'

'Yes, a pizza, please, and biscuits and crisps. Can I have some Coke too?'

'I'm not buying biscuits. We can make some cookies this evening. As for Coke, you're pushing your luck! I know your mother would never allow you to have it.'

'She does if it's Diet Coke.'

'Even worse!'

'Well then, what's the point of asking me what I want if everything I suggest is on your banned list?'

'I'm sure we can run to crisps and pizzas, and some pesto that you like. We can get some nice cheese, too.'

'Can you put a small carton of live yoghurt on the list?' Grandad asked. 'I want to make a big batch of yoghurt.'

'Why do you make your own yoghurt?' I asked.

'Homemade is much nicer, no additives, and besides, we make four pints at a time in a reusable pot, and don't have all that plastic to throw away from empty yoghurt cartons. One little pot will keep us going for months as we save a bit from every batch to use with the next one. You can help me if you like. I'll show you how,' Grandad said.

'I reckon a chocolate cake is on the cards, too,' Nan said.

Nan wrote 'chocolate' on the list, and self-raising flour.

'Can we have ice-cream? I'd love some Ben & Jerry's.'

'Oh, we'll make that ourselves, we just need some cream and there'll be plenty of eggs. The hens are laying well, and we've got some frozen raspberries from last year.'

'Silly me, of course you'd make your own ice-cream.'

'I've got a few jobs to do before we go. Molly, would you go out into the garden and pick some tulips? I want to drop some off at Mrs Frampton's on the way. She's having to isolate because of her age and her family are all down south. We can leave them on her doorstep with half a dozen eggs and give her a wave through the window. I want to check she's OK.'

I found the tulips, and as I bent down to pick them, I

66

spotted something small and brown, huddled down in the ground. I ran into the kitchen.

'I've found something. Come and see!' I motioned for Nan to come quietly, and I took her to the patch of tulips, gently pulling back the leaves.

'Ah, that's a leveret,' Nan said, 'a baby hare. Wonderful creatures. Hares often come into your life when you need to work something out.'

'I'll go and get Grandad!'

'No, we'll just keep this to ourselves, Molly. Hares are strongly feminine in their energy. Besides, Grandad won't want hares in the garden, nibbling his cabbages.'

*

We set off to town in their old blue van. I was surprised it was still going. They'd had it for as long as I could remember. It had a chimney poking out of the top and a wood-burning stove in the back. Grandad had converted it into a camper himself, and they took it to festivals. They'd once driven all the way around Spain and Portugal in it, taking my mam with them when she was tiny. It had red velvet curtains at the windows and a big sun sticker with a face that said 'Nuclear Power, No Thanks'. It had three seats across the front, and you had to climb up to get in it. I sat in between Nan and Grandad, high up in the cab. You could see right over the tops of the dry-stone walls.

The roads may have been quiet, but we weren't. The crockery and cutlery rattled in the cupboards, and Nan and Grandad were in fine voice.

We sang along to Bob Marley at full volume, his voice coming from speakers in the doors played from a cassette player in the dashboard. I didn't know anyone else who used cassettes. We laughed and sang, and for a while I forgot about everything bad. I looked across at Grandad, driving, at the wrinkles on his face, the tufts of hair coming out of his ears, the whiskers on his unshaven chin, and leant my head on his shoulder.

'Alright, duck?'

'Yes, just fine.'

When we got to Tesco the car park was heaving. People were coming out of the store with trollies piled high. Nearly everyone had toilet paper, balanced on the top, sometimes three packs on a trolley.

'Why on earth are people buying so much toilet paper?' I asked. 'Does Covid give you the runs?'

'It's because it said on the news that people were panic-buying toilet paper, so everyone rushes out and buys it even more!'

'You'll just use leaves, I suppose?'

'Very funny, Molly. No, I hope we can get some too.'

We queued for ages to get in, everyone spaced out in a long line that snaked around the car park. Some people were wearing masks. You could feel the panic in the air. When we got up to the door, a security guard stopped us.

'Only one person at a time allowed in the store. No family groups.'

'I'll go,' Grandad said. 'You wait in the van or have a walk down at Tyne Green.'

'But I need, well—'

'It's OK, Molly. You can tell Grandad what you need.

He's fine with buying period products. He won't bat an eyelid.'

'Erm, a packet of Always Ultra – the green pack.'

Grandad set off, pulling an old tartan shopping trolley on wheels behind him, and joined the queue. Mam just bought my pads in the weekly shop. It felt odd telling Grandad what I wanted, but then again, why the hell not? They could be so old-fashioned at times, but then again, so right on, too.

'Have you ever thought about a moon cup, Mollie?'

'Yeah, my friend Isabel from drama club uses one. Seems a bit gross, having to wash it out and all that, and what if it leaks?'

'I know several younger women who use them without any bother. So much more environmentally friendly. Your monthly blood is something to be celebrated, Molly, not shied away from! You know, we have a septic tank at home so follow the "Three Ps" rule with waste.'

'Dare I ask what the "Three Ps" are?'

'Poo, pee and paper,' Nan said.

'What do I do with used pads?'

'We'll have to bag them and put them in the general waste for now.'

Grandad was gone ages. We went for a walk along the river at Tyne Green; there were loads of people out and about. Boris Johnson had said we were allowed out to go shopping or to have daily exercise for an hour a day. There were people running, cycling and walking. I'd never seen it so busy down there. It was strange, though; everyone was giving each other a wide berth. If anyone stopped to chat, they stood feet apart. Some people were wearing masks. The playpark which was usually full of noisy kids was roped off with red and white plastic security tape. The café that sold ice-creams and teas was shut, and the tables piled up by the wall. Nan went to use the public toilets, but she found these shut too.

'Oh, gawd, where are we meant to have a wee?'

'You'll just have to wait until we get home.'

'You sound just like your mother,' Nan said, disappearing behind a bush. Sometimes she could be so embarrassing.

*

We all made a point of washing our hands when we got back. 'I've bought you an early birthday present,' Grandad said, handing over a box. It was a pair of purple spotty slippers.

'Brilliant! Thank you, Grandad. Purple too, my colour.' I hugged him then took a photo and sent it to Mam.

I offered to cook lunch and made proper pasta and pesto with grated cheddar on top. It was just what I needed. After lunch, Grandad went to his shed. He said I wasn't allowed in there and winked.

'Erm, I think I'll take Meg for a walk,' I said.

'Really?' Nan said. 'Shouldn't you be getting on with some schoolwork?'

'I did some earlier. It's fine, I just fancy a walk.'

'But it looks like rain.'

'I'm fine, don't fuss! I'm not made of sugar, as you so often say!'

Nan lent me a raincoat – it was huge, but I didn't care; no one would see me.

'Do you have any spare walking boots? My Docs gave me a blister yesterday, and they're getting ruined with all this mud.'

'Sure, there's an old pair of mine here. I reckon we're about the same size. I'll get you some thick socks in case they're too big.'

I pulled on a pair of stripy handknitted socks and tried on the walking boots. They felt great. The comfiest shoes I'd ever worn. I felt taller in them too.

I went in through the woods on the top path, this time. It was dark, where the trees were dense, but it kept the rain off. I trod quietly, trying not to make too much noise. The forest was silent. I went through the narrow gap in the trees, then ducked under a fallen tree that was covered in ivy. There was a gap in the ivy, and I parted it like curtains and stepped through.

Just ahead was a girl, crouched down low, picking wild garlic leaves. I thought it was the same girl I'd seen from the bridge.

I whispered, 'Shh,' to Meg, stroking the fur on her neck to calm her and slipped the lead on, then signalled for her to sit with a raised hand. I could see the girl's clothes better now: she was wearing a long green cloak with a hood and a long, brown, thick skirt, which was caked in mud. As she stood, the hood of the cloak fell back, and I saw that her hair was almost black, dirty and matted, the ends like dreadlocks, and had twigs and leaves stuck to it.

Meg whined and the girl looked up. Her skin was dark, but I couldn't get a proper look. We stood for the tiniest second looking at each other before she darted off towards the riverbank and the island. I called after her,

'Hey, don't be afraid!' then followed and watched her hop over the stones onto the bank opposite. I crossed the river too. It wasn't deep, and there were rocks just under the water where you could put your feet, although they were green and slippery. By the time I was across, I'd lost her. The bushes were thick and there didn't look to be a path, unlike on the other side, where the dogwalkers had worn a wide path through the woods.

Both Meg and I jumped when, from nowhere, the girl appeared in front of us.

She said nothing. Just looked at me. Stared. She looked dead rough. She looked younger than me, but it was hard to tell. She was skinny, and a good bit shorter. She was filthy! Her skin looked awful, with spots and blackheads and streaks of dirt. What a freak!

'Hi,' I said. She said nothing. *Rude as well as filthy*, I thought.

She was staring at the moon I'd found and tied around my wrist.

'Is this yours? I found it by the log seat,' I said, taking it off and holding it out.

The girl snatched it and held it to her heart.

With that, she disappeared, back through a tangle of bushes and branches.

She was well weird. I wondered if I should follow her. From the state of her it looked like she'd been sleeping rough for a while. I wondered if I should tell Nan about her, or Mam, or the police? She was obviously in trouble, big trouble. Something in my gut told me I should keep shtum, though.

Eight

Molly and Martha

I felt responsible: couldn't get the girl from the woods out of my mind. Was she a missing person? Where had she come from? Were her parents looking for her? Why was she in such a state? What should I do about it all? I nearly said something at one point over breakfast. Luckily though, Nan nicked off early and Grandad did his usual disappearing act outside. Nan was off on her rounds, on her bike. As well as having people knocking on the door, she delivered her herbal teas and remedies to people round and about. Wasn't she supposed to stay at home? We were in lockdown, but Nan was having none of it.

'We can call it my daily exercise,' she said. 'And besides, I only leave things on people's doorsteps. You could say I was an essential worker.'

I laughed. Yes, I supposed she was.

I had a missed call from my form tutor, so I thought

I'd better get on with some schoolwork. I put my phone on silent. The group chat would have to wait even though it had been pinging all morning. The teachers were sending emails, and we were told we had to go on Google Classroom to get work and upload what we'd done. Some of my friends from drama club went to the posh school in town and they had to turn up for registration on Zoom at 9am and work until 3pm in their school uniforms. Our school wasn't that bad, and I was glad I didn't have to face Jess and the others. We had a drama club Zoom on Wednesday night, but that would be OK. None of the beautiful people went to drama club. At drama club it was OK to be different. You could just be yourself. I didn't bother straightening my hair or wearing loads of makeup there. I could even have turned up in Nan's jumper and no one would bat an eyelid.

I did a bit of English; we had been reading *Lord of the Flies* and had to discuss the characters in the story. I wrote about Piggy, and how he was an outsider, different from the other boys. He'd been brought up by his auntie and wasn't one of the cool kids. You never learnt Piggy's real name but knew he was fat. I wrote about how the other kids only saw the fat, his glasses and asthma, and didn't look beyond that. He also didn't behave like the rest of the boys, and that set him apart. He wasn't one of the gang. As I wrote I thought about how I was different. I didn't always get the jokes or know what to say. I looked down at my stomach. Was I fat? I always thought I was. My mam had me watching my weight all the time, but did I really look so bad? I had no idea.

I worked for about half an hour then checked my notifications. Mam had messaged to nag me about working, and I assured her I was. I asked her how she was. 'Fine,' she said, but I didn't believe her. I'd seen on social media and on the news about the lack of PPE, how the nurses were having to wear bin liners instead of aprons, how there was a massive shortage of face masks, and about the soaring rates of infection and people dying of this virus. I had watched clips of nurses in tears, exhausted. I hoped she was OK. I told her I was thinking of her.

I worked until lunchtime and then made a sandwich and wandered out into the garden to find Grandad. I could hear his wood lathe and the chisel as it carved into the wood.

'Hi, Grandad, I've made you a cheese and chutney sandwich,' I called from the door. I had to shout to be heard above the noise of the machine.

'Hang on!' He turned off the lathe and covered what he was making with a cloth. 'OK, you can come in!' Grandad sat down in the armchair next to the wood burner. It was cosy in there. 'Ooft, I'm tired,' he said, groaning as he eased himself into the chair.

We ate our sandwiches together and chatted. I loved being in here with the smell of wood. Grandad could tell what tree the wood had come from just by looking at it. There was a sign on the road, 'Crafts for Sale', and a table in the shed with wooden spoons, bowls, walking sticks and some of Nan's knitted things and paintings.

'We'll not be selling much during lockdown, Molly.'

'Have you ever thought of selling online?'

'Oh, I wouldn't know where to start. I know your nan has Facebook, but all that's a different world to me.'

'I could help! I'd love to. We'd need to photograph your

things and then make an online shop. My friend Emma's mam sells her sea glass jewellery on Etsy. I'll ask her what's the best way of doing it.'

'Well, that would be grand, Molly. But, if you don't mind, I think I'll have forty winks while your nan's out of the way.' Grandad did look pale and tired all of a sudden, so I left him to rest.

*

With Nan out on her errands and Grandad in the land of nod, I thought it was a good time to head to the shop to stock up and see if I could find the girl again. There were a thousand questions buzzing around my head. I wanted to know what was going on, if she needed help and why she was dressed in those odd clothes, looking like she hadn't had a wash in months. Surely someone must be worried about her other than me? I didn't take Meg with me this time; she was fast asleep by Grandad's feet and didn't seem to want to leave him.

There were more people out today, more walkers than I'd ever seen. All getting their hour's exercise. At the shop, there was a table across the door to stop people going in, and Martin was stood behind. There was a bottle of hand sanitiser and Martin had a plastic visor over his face. I reached in my pocket for my mask. Nan had made one for each of us, cutting up an old skirt and lining it with material from a pillowcase. There were disposable masks for sale at the shop. I'd noticed a blue and white mask dropped along the lane. Not exactly environmentally friendly, I'd thought. Maybe Nan and I could make some

76

more and drop them off at the shop? I laughed. My nan's influence was rubbing off on me.

Outside the shop people queued, all spaced apart. The vicar was waiting in queue, his dog collar and his height singling him out from everyone else. He was grey-haired, had mean-looking eyes and a face like a wet weekend.

'It's Molly, isn't it?'

'Yes, I'm staying with Nan and Grandad during lockdown.'

'Hmm, I hope your nan's behaving herself.'

'Does she ever?' I joked, but I didn't like the look on his face. What was that supposed to mean? Dad had once said her all-night house parties were legendary, and I know she went to illegal raves back in the eighties and night clubs in the nineties. The oldest raver in town! Except it wasn't town, was it? It was no more than a poxy little village where everyone seemed to know everyone else's business.

With my bag full of sweets, crisps and pop, I headed back over the green bridge. I spotted the girl a good way off in the distance, down by the bank. She was in the water, bent over with both hands in the shallows, her skirt hooked up at the sides.

I took the path along the riverbank. A good way in, I saw her again. I stayed back and watched her step on rocks that jutted out of the water, hitching her skirt with one hand, carrying a basket with two fish in it on her hip with the other.

She must have known I was following her, because once she was across the water, she turned and with a slight nod of her head, beckoned for me to follow. The stones were green with slime, and I wondered how she hadn't slipped and fallen in, I nearly did. In the air there was a smell of woodsmoke, and in a small clearing, there was a fire and a rough shelter made from branches, covered with moss and ivy. She bent down to the fire, poked it and added more sticks. Standing, she faced me.

'I saw you on the bridge.'

'Oh, how embarrassing. I'm sorry. I'd lost the plot.'

'Lost what?'

'The plot. I get really upset sometimes. It's a long story. You see, I live in town, in Newcastle. That is, I did, before the pandemic. I was meant to go back there this weekend. It is my birthday on Saturday, and I was going to go out with my friends. We had a table booked at Wagamama and everything. Was going to get my nails done, go birthday shopping. Was even going to get my bellybutton pierced. That's all on hold now.'

'Newcastle?'

'Yeah, I live there with my mam. In Heaton, know it? She's a nurse at the RVI and is busy, what with the pandemic and everything, so now I'm stuck here with my nan and grandad.'

The girl just stood there, looking at me, her head on one side. She looked really confused. A dog barked over in the nature reserve and the girl ducked down, beckoning me to do the same. She held her finger to her lips. A guy was calling his dog: 'Wilson! Come!' There was a high-pitched dog whistle and lots of barking. Then they were gone. The girl's eyes were out on stalks, her breathing rapid. I was sure now she was on the run.

'It's OK, they're gone. No one comes over here. They just stick to the path through the woods and back over the green bridge. The dogwalkers, that is. My grandad hates them, hanging their plastic dog poo bags on the branches.'

The girl looked puzzled.

'I'm Molly, by the way.'

She didn't say anything, so I tried again. 'You can speak English, can't you? My name's Molly, what's yours?'

'Martha.'

'Here, let's do a selfie. Smile.'

Martha looked a bit bewildered, but I snapped a photo. This would be something to show the others. She was such a minger!

'Well, Martha, what's going on?'

'I am in fear.'

'You what?'

'I am in fear, I am in hiding.'

'Yeah, well, I gathered that. Who from? Have you run away?'

'They took my mother.'

'Who took your mother? Where is she?'

Martha's voice cracked as she spoke, and she fiddled with the moon on her wrist. 'I believe she is in the gaol. I didn't know what to do. She told me to hide, to run, to trust no one.'

'You can trust me.'

'Pray thee, can I?'

Martha started sobbing. Tears were falling down her face, making streaks in the dirt on her face. She wiped snot on the back of her sleeve. She really was gross.

'Here, have a tissue,' I said, offering her some, wondering about the weird lingo, all these 'pray thees' and such.

She stared at the packet, stroking the plastic with her finger. She was one strange girl, with her weird clothes, strange language, foraged food and wild camping. I wondered what her story was. She looked half starved and didn't smell that good either. I presumed she was homeless.

'Here, want some Haribo?' I said, getting a packet out of my bag.

She looked at the packet but didn't take any. Maybe she was foreign. Perhaps they didn't have Haribo where she came from. Nah, everyone had Haribo! They had them in Greece when we went on holiday last year. I opened the packet and handed it to her. She took one and held it up to the light. I ate a fistful, and she popped a couple of gummy bears into her mouth. Saliva ran down her chin and a smile spread on her face.

'Why don't you come back with me? I'm sure Nan wouldn't mind. It's nearly teatime. The food's not great, but it's better than nothing.'

'No! You must go now! Means, go!'

'Suit yourself.' I turned to leave, parting the bushes to make my way back to the bank, then turned. 'I'll come back tomorrow, bring you some proper food.'

'God spede you.'

*

I checked to see no one was watching me crossing the water and walked back through the woods deep in thought. I had so many questions, and she really needed help. I'd go back tomorrow and find out more. I added the photo I'd taken to my Instagram stories, but when I did, it was only of me. The weirdo wasn't on it! That was nuts. I'd try again when I got back.

On the top of the hill, by the big oak tree, the setting sun cast a golden glow on the tower of the farm, and you could see the light reflecting on the river. It looked like a silver snake. I looked up at huge oak tree, at its thick, strong branches, and remembered climbing it with my dad when we I was a kid, sitting in the bowl in the middle. I made a mental note to give him a ring later, and Mam, I'd ring her too. I wondered whether to tell her about Martha. Probably not. There was something about all this that felt kind of delicate, like I needed to tread carefully. As I was thinking about Mam, I caught a flash of something silver out of the corner of my eye, and then there was the brown hare again, the setting sun making it look like it had a ring of light around it. It was sitting by an old stone gate post next to a rusted metal gate. When I walked past, I spotted some silver threads caught on the bottom rung of the gate. They looked out of place, amongst the grasses and wildflowers. I bent down and pulled them off, then held them across my palm. The light caught them, and they sparkled, and as they did the hairs on my arms rose. I had no idea why. I popped them in my pocket. Just as I turned the corner, two young deer jumped over the wall and away across the field, their white rumps bobbing up and down. There might not be many shops, but the wildlife took my breath away.

'Ah, there you are! I was wondering where you'd got to!' Nan was stirring a large pan on the Rayburn when I went in. 'I'm batch-cooking lentil and vegetable soup for the freezer. Do you want some?'

'Yes, I don't mind if I do.'

Nan raised her eyebrows and smiled, and I got some spoons and bowls ready for the table. I sat down and tried uploading the photo again. I was in it, there were the trees and the woods, but where was Martha? She had been right next to me when I'd taken it. Well odd. I tried again. Same.

I gave up and I checked the group chat. Oh great, Jess had posted the picture I'd sent her of me in the jumper Nan had given me.

just look at the state of Molly. what's she wearing? height of fashion as ever! pmsl 😂

omg what a freak 🐷 how fat does she look in that? pmsl 😺

ya, ginger hair and with those sleeves she looks like an orangutan 🦧🦧🦧🦧🦧

what a ginga! 😄🦧🦧🦧😄

ya, well at least she's outta the picture now 🦧 ☺

yeah, lucky escape that 😅

gone to her weird grandparents 👵 👴 her nan's a witch 🧹 has seances 🐵

you'd better watch out Jess, she might turn you into a toad 🐸

er, Jess, I think Molly's part of this group?

nah, I don't think so. pretty sure I wouldn't have added her!

just checked the list – she is

f*ck! my bad! 😵 🥴

doubt she's seeing this. too busy eating cake 🍰 and casting spells 🧹 🧙

The total bitch! I'd only sent the jumper picture to Jess for a laugh. How dare she?

'Molly!' Nan interrupted.

'What?' I said, not meaning to sound as impatient as I did.

'Molly, are you OK?'

What was this, the Spanish inquisition?

'No. I'm not,' I snapped, and slammed my phone down on the table.

'Why don't you leave your phone and go and call Grandad in for supper? Whatever has happened, it can't be as bad as all that.'

'Can you just leave me alone?' I said, trying not to cry.

'Molly? You'll break your phone! Enough of your tantrums. Now, could you go and call your grandad. Please?'

I shoved my chair back hard, went to the back door and yelled for Grandad. I was so angry. I yelled again, but there was no reply, so I went outside, slamming the back door as I went. They were supposed to be my friends! I should never have sent the photo to Jess in the first place. Jess! After all we've been through. How dare she? What a cow! What was I thinking? I thought it was funny, just a laugh. How could they be so cruel? As for Gareth and the lads. I was mortified. It was dark, and the cold air felt good. I didn't go straight to the workshop. I went down to the burn and stood watching the water for a while. My head was a jumble of thoughts. One thing was for sure. I had no friends. I didn't want to see any of them ever again.

I'd pinched a couple of rizlas and some baccy off Grandad and rolled a ciggie. As soon as I lit up, I regretted it. Instant tobacco rush that made me feel car-sick. I kept trying but couldn't get the hang of smoking. After a while I tuned in to the noise the flowing water was making. My heart stopped thudding in my chest. I dried my eyes, blew my nose and headed over to the workshop. It was dark in there. I could just make out the shape of Grandad still in his chair by the log burner. It must have gone out. It was freezing. Meg was laid by his feet.

'Grandad! Wake up, supper's ready.'

Grandad opened his eyes and lifted his head slowly. He started coughing.

'Are you OK?'

'No, duck, I don't feel that good.'

'You don't look great. I'll go and get Nan.'

'It's OK, I'm awake now. Don't get too close, though. I think I'm going down with something.'

Act Two

Pink Moon

Nine

Outsiders

For a moment when I woke up, warm under the duvet, everything felt OK. But then I remembered. Not only had I made a right idiot of myself and was now the butt of everyone's jokes, but I was in exile down a muddy lane, living in the dark ages. My mam was fighting a killer disease, and might even catch it herself, and now Grandad was sick. What if he'd caught the virus somehow? That was too horrid to think of. I reached for my phone. There were fifteen notifications. I opened them up then instantly regretted it. It was like picking at a spot. You know it is only going to make it worse, but you can't resist. The lads were having a pile-on. Rude comments about rather seeing me without my jumper and about the size of my boobs and what they'd like to do with them. Jess had sent several messages saying she didn't mean it and it was only a laugh. Some joke! Esmée was asking if I was OK, and that she was there for me. The two-faced cow! I'd seen her join in with the others, slagging me off.

I put my phone down and turned over in bed. The sunlight was pricking through the thin curtains and the same bird as yesterday was letting rip in the tree outside. I wondered what bird it was – what was so important that it had to make all that noise? As I listened to it the noises in my own head got smaller. Maybe there was an app for identifying birdsong? I picked up my phone to search for one but threw it down on the bed as it pinged again.

Yesterday's clothes were on the floor: the jumper Nan had made me and my black leggings. I put them on then sniffed my socks – they'd do. I couldn't be bothered having a shower or doing my hair, so pulled it back into a bobble.

Downstairs, wedges of sunshine full of dancing dust sliced through the kitchen. Nan was already up. Did she ever go to bed? She had her back to me, making a plopping noise with a wooden spoon in an old-fashioned mixing bowl. Her butt cheeks wobbled as she mixed and moved in time to the music from the radio. She was dressed head to toe in purple, and I mean head to toe. A purple and gold scarf was wound around her hair, which looked even more orange as the sunlight hit it through the window. She was wearing a purple and green hippy top with swirling patterns, and her fat ankles bulged from purple leggings, and on her feet were purple Crocs. She should come with a government health warning and a pair of sunglasses: 'Looking at this woman could seriously damage your eyes.'

'Pancakes for breakfast!' she announced, brandishing her wooden spoon in the air as pancake mixture flicked onto the wall. Where did she get her energy from?

'How's Grandad this morning?' I asked.

'He's up and in his workshop. Was coughing a bit but said he wanted to get on. He never likes staying in bed.' I wondered if getting up at the crack of dawn was a thing all old people did, or was it just these two barking nutters?

The pancakes were wonderful: warm and fluffy, just what I needed. Nan poured rosehip syrup on them which she'd made herself. It was delicious. Just the carb and sugar hit I needed.

'I might take Meggie for a walk after breakfast.' I had to go and check on Martha. See if she was still there or if she had run off.

'You're very keen on walking all of a sudden, Molly. Are you sure it's not an avoidance tactic so you don't have to do your schoolwork?' Nan sat down and tucked into the pancakes with me.

I speared another pancake and drenched it in syrup. 'Nah, I'll do some later. There's someone…' I couldn't decide if I should tell Nan about Martha or not. Every time it was on the tip of my tongue, something stopped me.

'We could go together,' said Nan, bulldozing her way in as usual. She had this habit of interrupting. 'I want to get some more coltsfoot. It's just started to flower, and I'm nearly out of my coltsfoot cough syrup. Your grandad could do with some.'

Now my phone was going ballistic.

'You're popular,' Nan said.

I put it on silent. 'Not really.'

'Must be hard, not seeing your friends. Are they missing you?'

'They can go to hell.'

Nan put her fork down, raised both eyebrows and looked at me over the top of her glasses. 'Strong words, Molly. Want to tell your nan what's going on?'

'Nah, I'm good, thanks.' Where would I even begin? I took another pancake even though I was getting full.

Nan looked at me for a minute, then turned away and picked up a glass jar from the windowsill that contained a manky mess of stalks and flowers. As she held it up to the light, the liquid shone a bright yellow. She seemed to sense all was not good with me, but I was glad she didn't push it.

'Where did you learn all this, Nan, all this herbal stuff? By the way, this rosehip syrup is delicious.' I reached for the bottle and poured a bit more.

'It's been passed down over generations, Molly. This is ancient knowledge, but I got most of it from my grandmother, and she from her mother.'

With that, Nan got up and went down the steps and into her workshop. I sat back and rubbed my belly. I was stuffed! I could hear her unlocking a cupboard, and she returned with a large brown book.

The book was old. It even smelt old, kind of musty. The pages were thin and yellowing around the edges. It was bound in leather and had a gold crescent moon on the cover. Nan turned the pages carefully.

'This was my grandmother's. It's been passed down through the family. Look, here's her drawing of the coltsfoot flower.'

I looked at the drawing – so delicate, and her handwriting, with its loops and swirls, the ink faded and brown. Little symbols and diagrams, with notes and her recipe for coltsfoot syrup. I ran my fingers gently over the page. The paper felt fragile, as thin as tissue paper in places.

'This book holds some the secrets to my nan's healing powers, and she left space so that I could add my own drawings and footnotes – see, I've put notes on where coltsfoot grows, and when it can be picked.'

Nan turned to another page with drawings of flowers, herbs and berries. They were beautifully drawn. Some of the writing was so old, I could hardly make it out at all. I got a strange feeling, holding this book, like electricity tingling through my fingers.

'This is amazing!' I placed the coltsfoot jar next to the book and set it up for a photo. It made a good flat lay. I thought I might post it on Insta.

'It is, isn't it? And one day it will be yours.'

'I used to love drawing but haven't done any lately. Never seem to have the time.'

'Well then, we'll have to get you started again. You've got plenty of time on your hands now – that is, if you ever put that phone of yours down!'

She had a point. I put it down. I wouldn't share that photo after all. I didn't want to give the gang any more reason to bitch about me.

'What was she like, your nan?'

Nan smiled and reached for an old black and white photo in a wooden frame that was sitting on the cupboard. It was of an old lady, dressed in baggy trousers and a man's shirt with a large straw hat on her head. She had a basket in her hand and was looking out across a garden.

'Oh, she was wonderful! Well, I thought she was wonderful, but there were many who didn't. She had a sharp tongue in her head and didn't hold back if she had an opinion about something. Fell out with a lot of folks.' *Now I know where she got it from*, I thought to myself, but didn't say out loud.

I was keen to get going and see Martha, but Nan was making a pot of tea and I was enjoying our chat.

'Tell me more about your nan. Sounds like you were close?'

Nan brought the teapot to the table, and two pretty cups and saucers with gold rims and little blue flowers.

'Nan always said that tea tastes so much better from a proper cup,' she said when she saw me looking at them. 'These cups and saucers were hers.' She popped a knitted tea cosy over the pot. 'Oh, Molly, she was my best friend in life. The person I went to when it all got too much. She was warm and jolly, and we had so much fun at her house. We dressed up, made dens and took all the cushions off her settee to jump on. My brother would go shooting pheasants in the woods with our grandad, not that we told our parents. We used to stay with them on weekends. We'd race down the alleyway to their house, the sound of our feet clattering off the brick walls, to be the first to get to the back door and into her arms. She gave the best hugs.'

'So that's where you get it from then?'

Nan smiled, lifted off the tea cosy and stirred the pot. She looked out of the window and continued, 'She had a big garden with a long wooden greenhouse and grew all her own herbs, vegetables and fruit. She had a little wooden table out the front of the house, where she sold spare produce: runner beans and tomatoes, trays of plants. I used to help, picking and putting vegetables in brown paper bags. The smell of a freshly picked ripe tomato takes me straight back to her. I still miss her, even though she died a long time ago. Sometimes, when I'm in our greenhouse I get the feeling she's just behind me.' There was a catch to Nan's voice, as if even after all these years, talking about her nan could make her cry.

'She sounds just like you. Shall I pour the tea?' I hunted for the tea strainer but couldn't find one. Nan was away down memory lane. The sun was pouring in through the window, and I was enjoying this time, just the two of us. I sat back, drank my tea and let her talk.

'Nan made jams and jellies, chutney and pickles, and we would spend hours picking blackberries or walking through the woods, looking for mushrooms in autumn or picking primroses in spring, tying them in little bunches on sticks. She taught me to love nature, to make simple remedies from the plants around us. She was a dab hand at telling fortunes too!'

'How? Did she read palms or have a crystal ball?'

'No, nothing like that. She did have a sixth sense, though. Often knew when things were going to happen. She read the tea leaves.'

'Tea leaves?'

She laughed. 'Oh, I remember when my nan into trouble for reading tea leaves in my parents' house.'

'What happened?'

'Well, my mother had gone out the room, and Nan said she'd tell my fortune. She looked at the pattern made by the tea leaves, then foretold I'd marry a tall, handsome man with sandy hair and have three children, which I did: your mother and her brothers. Then my mother came back in the room and all merry hell broke loose!'

'Why? What was wrong with that?'

'Oh, my mother and father had gone and got religion bad. They didn't approve of fortune-telling or horoscopes. They said it was the work of the Devil.'

'Well, she was right – you did marry someone tall and have three children!'

I hadn't seen Uncle Andrew or Uncle Paul since my cousin Sally's wedding when Nan disgraced herself according to Mam. Something about getting too drunk and having an outside wee in the hotel's ornamental garden at the wedding reception. Uncle Andrew lived in London with his husband, and Uncle Paul lived on a houseboat so was always moving around. Neither had any kids, so I was Nan and Grandad's only granddaughter.

'What does my cup say?'

'Let's see. Drink up but leave the dregs at the bottom.'

Nan showed me her cup with the remainder of tea in the bottom and tea leaves floating in it. Then she swirled it around three times and tipped it upside down on the saucer.

'There, now you do the same, Molly.'

'Is this right?' The cup felt delicate in my hands, the handles so small. I was afraid of breaking it.

'Yes, and don't forget to ask it a question as you turn it upside down. The tea leaves may well give you the answer you are looking for.'

'One, two, three.' I swirled the cup and turned it upside down on the saucer. It made me think of blowing out candles on a cake and making a wish. I had a lot of questions I could have asked but settled on one.

Nan went quiet and studied the leaves that were stuck

around the cup. She looked up at me, then looked back at the tea leaves. Her face didn't give anything away.

'What? What do you see?' I couldn't see anything apart from tea leaves stuck to the cup.

'There is a bird, see?' Nan pointed to a clump of tea leaves near the top of the cup. 'A journey, maybe, a flight, escape of some kind, freedom. There is a tree too, which suggests strength. There is a cross – look, trouble ahead. Maybe trouble with love, with a boy?'

This was nuts. How could Nan see all that from a few leaves?

'What is important to remember, Molly, is that there is no real power in the leaves, just reflections of what is already inside of you. It is important to trust your own instincts, your gut feelings. Follow your own journey and do what you believe is right.'

She could be dead deep at times, my nan. I had no idea how I should reply to that so got up and cleared the table, stacking the plates by the sink.

'You know, Molly, whatever is going on with you and your friends, you can tell your old nan. I may be getting on a bit, but I've had a past too.'

I didn't doubt that for a minute! I knew Nan had been out there, going to festivals and having all-night parties and raves. I liked that about her. She wasn't your typical grandma. OK, she did knit and do other granny stuff, but she had a wild streak. I turned on the hot tap and reached for the washing-up liquid.

'Come on, Molly, leave those. Let's get some fresh air. We'll check on your grandad on the way and I'll show you where the coltsfoot grows.'

*

'Ye gods, you look dreadful!' Nan exclaimed when we went into Grandad's workshop. He was leaning on both hands, head bent over his workbench.

Nan pulled an old chair behind Grandad, put her hands on his shoulders. 'Joe, sit down!' Nan said rather sharply, and he sat down with a heavy thump as she pushed him into the chair. There were beads of sweat on his bald head which he wiped with his woolly hat. What hair he did have stuck to his head in a wet clump. He didn't look right at all. He'd gone a very funny colour.

'I'm fine. It's nothing.'

'For goodness' sake, why don't you take it easy?' Nan said. 'It's no wonder you've caught a chill, spending all day in this freezing workshop. Molly and I are just off to pick some coltsfoot and then we'll be straight back to make some lentil soup for lunch.'

'I won't want any lunch.'

'What do you mean, you won't want any lunch?'

'Just what I say, I don't want any lunch.'

'Don't be ridiculous, Joe. You need to eat!'

'Can't you leave me alone, woman? I feel a bit queasy, that's all, and like I said, I don't want any lunch. Now, if you don't mind, I'd rather be left in peace. I've got a heap of things to do. The peas and beans need sowing, and there's something I want to finish here.'

Grandad looked in my direction and winked. I guessed Grandad was making me something for my birthday. He'd made me wooden toys when I was little: a pull-along elephant, building blocks, even a doll's house, every room

96

full of handmade furniture. Mam had given it away when we moved, which was OK, I suppose. We'd never have fitted it into the flat.

'Well then, I'm going to get that stove going, Grandad, you need to keep warm.' I picked up some sticks and went to open the log burner.

'It's OK, Molly, I can manage.'

'Stubborn as ever!' Nan said, raising her eyes and shaking her head. 'Come on, Molly, we'll leave him to it.'

It wasn't like Grandad to be this tetchy.

Then a horrid thought crashed in my head and my stomach lurched. What if Grandad really did have Covid? What if it was all my fault, for being fussy and wanting pizzas and ice-cream? My heart started beating faster. I'd never forgive myself if it was my fault Grandad was ill. What if Grandad died and it was all my fault?

Ten

Kindred Spirits

We both seemed deep in thought and for a while walked side by side in silence.

'You must be worried about Grandad,' I said to Nan.

'Oh, he'll be OK. He always gets allergies this time of year. Hay fever knocks him for six every time the sloe blossom appears. Look!'

Nan pointed to the little white flowers, and I thought back to that walk with Grandad down the lane when I first arrived.

'He also needs to stop smoking!' Nan said. 'He thinks I don't know, sneaking off to his shed like he does, but I can smell it on him. I'm not daft.'

Nan might have been right about Grandad having a smoker's cough and having allergies. I hoped so but wasn't convinced.

Meg, without a care in world, was trotting happily in

front, tail swishing from side to side, turning every now and then to check we were still there. The sky was blue, it was warm, and it wasn't long before Nan and I both took off our coats. In the distance, the farmer's quad could be heard checking on sheep that were due to lamb. I used to help with feeding the pet lambs up at the farm before the big fallout with Mam and Nan and Grandad. They'd need to be bottle-fed. I smiled as I remembered how hard they sucked, and the fight there was to hold on to the bottle. They were very cute. I wondered if I'd be able to help again, or if Covid and lockdown meant we had to keep clear?

I was still thinking about whether to tell Nan about Martha. I kept changing my mind. If she reported her to the police, then it might make things worse for her, but then again, maybe Martha did need professional help, a social worker, perhaps? I decided at that moment that I would tell her. I trusted that Nan would do the right thing. I'd show her Martha's camp and see if I could get her to persuade her to come and stay with us.

'Listen,' Nan said, stopping suddenly.

'I can't hear anything, just the birds.'

'That's just it. You can't usually hear them above the A69 and the thrum of traffic. Your grandad hates it, says he's going to blow up that road one day. It's gone quiet.'

'What are those birds?' I said, looking across the field which was full of black and white birds with orange beaks and feet.

'Oyster catchers. They come back every spring. Aren't they wonderful? Seems this lockdown has hidden blessings. It's as if nature is being amplified and man's destruction toned down.'

As we stood there watching the birds, a sleek train of blue and grey metal sliced through the green of the fields and trees. It was on its way to Newcastle, and I thought of my life there and what it would have been like in lockdown. Boris Johnson had said you could only exercise for an hour a day from your home so that ruled out going any further than walking around Heaton Park or down Chillingham Road. Drinking cheap cider and smoking stolen tabs on the Town Moor had somehow lost its allure.

*

We carried on walking, then turned in by the green bridge, following the riverbank where trees and bushes grew, some of them dipping their leaves into the water. After while Nan said she needed a rest, so we sat down on a sandy bank by the water's edge. The river was wide, moving slowly, and I tossed a stick into the water for Meg, who swam, doggy paddle, out to fetch it, then brought it back to my feet, shaking river water over our legs.

'Nan, can I ask you something?'

'Fire away, poppet.'

I stood up and hurled Meg's stick as far as I could into the water, then sat back down. 'What were you like when you were a teenager? Did you have lots of friends?'

'No, I didn't, as a matter of fact. Was a bit of an outsider. Why do you ask? Am I right in thinking you've had a falling-out with your friends?'

'I thought they were friends, but I'm not so sure now. You know this jumper you gave me? Don't get me wrong,

I love it, but my friends have been taking the mickey out of me for wearing it.'

'Is that all? Ignore them, Molly, they're just jealous they don't have a nan who knits such fabulous creations! Besides, wouldn't they rather have something made with love and natural fibres than some nasty piece of man-made, throwaway fashion?'

'No, they're not jealous. And no, they wouldn't wear a multicoloured stripy jumper made from wool. Jess said she wouldn't be seen dead in it. They've been rude about you too, and that isn't all. There's other stuff.'

'What "other stuff"?' Nan asked.

I wanted to talk to Nan about the whole friendship thing but wasn't sure how much or what I wanted to say. I decided to skirt around the issue for a while. 'Nan, why do you say you were you an outsider? Didn't you have friends? Was it because you were a hippy back then, like you are now?'

Nan laughed, then went deadly serious. She fiddled with her hair, taking a clump of her fringe and twirling it around her finger as she spoke. 'I didn't have what my parents called "secular" friends. Our family only really mixed with church people.'

'OMG! That sounds hideous! What about school? Didn't you have school friends?'

'I had one good friend, Anne. I never really managed to make friends with anyone else; never knew what to say or what to talk about. I found it hard being part of any groups. I was the odd one out, with my sensible shoes and Jesus stickers on my tan leather briefcase when everyone else had platforms and PVC tote bags with Martini and Cinzano emblems.'

101

I listened and Nan carried on: 'Sundays were all about church, and I worked on a Saturday. I didn't hang out with friends or go to sleepovers, and I certainly wasn't allowed to go to parties or discos, so my friend and I stuck together. Kindred spirits, I guess. I keep in touch with her now. Your mam's middle name is Anne, after her. We got up to some things together! We were wild, I can tell you, not that our parents knew the half of it. We'd pretend we were staying at each other's houses and then go out on the town, picking lads up who were often much older than us. I shudder to think of some of the places we ended up at and the states we got ourselves in.'

'I got myself in a bit of a state at a party too.'

'I'm guessing drink was involved? Drugs?'

'No drugs, but I drank far too much. Ended up in a bedroom with a lad.'

I remembered waking up on top of a single bed in a strange room, the smell of peach schnapps and vomit making me retch and want to throw up. As I heaved over the side of the bed, I realised that it was me who had been sick on the carpet there already. My pants were down and around one of my ankles.

'Do you want to tell me what happened?' Nan asked. 'You won't shock me, you know, and it won't go any further.'

For a minute I felt like crying. 'If I'm honest, I don't really know what happened. I remember Gareth shouting at me and slamming the door on his way out. I must have passed out. And now he's going around telling all his mates I had sex with him, and I'm pretty sure I didn't. Well, I don't think I did. Now everyone is calling me a slag and I don't want to show my face ever again at school.'

'I'm guessing your mother doesn't know any of this?'

'I could never tell her! She'd kill me! You won't tell Mam, will you? You said it wouldn't go any further!'

'No, it won't, Molly, but you underestimate your mam. Sometimes, when someone is hurting, they put down the shutters, act angry or put up barriers to stop themselves being damaged any more. Try talking to her. You may be surprised.'

I hadn't thought of Mam hurting. I thought she was just in a permanent grump because Dad had left. I'd always thought it was her nagging and bad moods that had driven Dad away. Maybe there was more to it.

'I just don't fit in. I feel like I'm always on the edge. I try so hard to be like the rest but just never seem to get it right.' Meg had slumped down next to me; her chin was on my legs and was making my leggings wet, but I didn't mind. Her body next to mine felt comforting. I put my hand on her back and could feel her panting.

'Sounds like you're trying too hard,' Nan said. 'Ever thought you don't need to fit in?'

'I don't know what you mean.'

'Well, do you really want to be just like them? Maybe it's OK just to be you.'

'What, short, fat Molly, the girl with frizzy hair that no one wants to be friends with? The class slag who'll do anything with anyone?'

'I think you need to learn to love yourself a bit more, Molly. It's important to have self-respect, set some boundaries. I learnt that one the hard way.'

'What do you mean? What happened, Nan?'

'Oh, you don't need to know the gory details, Molly.

I was desperate to be loved and went about it in all the wrong ways. I knew nothing about self-respect and ended up being very hurt. It wasn't until I met your grandad that I began to learn that I was good enough, and that I didn't have anything to prove. It's been a long journey, mind you. It's taken me years to find out who I really am, get over the mistakes I made and learn to like, never mind love myself.'

I handed Nan a tissue. Tears were falling down her face. She blew her nose. My nan, who usually looked so bold and brave, looked crumpled and small. I didn't know what to say but put my arm around her shoulder.

'Grandad will be OK, Nan. We'll look after him.'

I stood up and threw Meg's stick into the water. She soon retrieved it and bounded up and out of the river, shaking sandy water all over us, making us laugh.

'Come on, pull your old nan up, this coltsfoot won't pick itself.' Nan held out her hand and I got up and tugged her up. We fell into a hug and stood there for a while on the bank, holding each other, rocking gently from side to side, while the river flowed silently past.

*

It's funny how, once you start to look for something, you see it everywhere. There were knobbly stalks with yellow flowers that looked like bright suns growing all along the riverbank. I picked a few and laid them gently in the wide wicker basket Nan had brought, careful not to damage them. Nan did the same and we soon had a basketful. It was so peaceful, with the sound of the river and the birds, and beautiful too with the sun reflecting off the water. I watched my nan, bent over with her huge backside in the air, and smiled. Who'd have thought picking weeds with a mad old crone could be this good?

'Cough wort,' a gentle voice said behind me. 'Does someone ail?'

I hadn't heard Martha come through the trees, but there she was. Brilliant! Decision made for me. Now Nan would meet Martha.

'Yes, it's my grandad,' I said. 'He's got this awful cough, and Nan thinks we should give him coltsfoot syrup. I've no idea how to make it but am helping her pick it.'

'Who are you talking to, Molly?' Nan called, looking up from where she was picking, further down the bank. 'I thought it was only me who talked to herself!'

Martha looked at me with wide eyes then shook her head and stepped back under cover of the trees. I had to think fast. 'I was talking to the dog. Fetch, Meggie!' I threw her stick along the ground, then whispered into the darkness, 'That's my nan, she's cool. You can trust her.'

But Martha had gone.

'Well, I'm heading back now, Molly,' Nan said, bustling along the bank. 'I want to get this coltsfoot into the tincture water while it's fresh. Are you coming?'

'If it's OK, I think I'll walk on a bit more. I've got some thinking to do.'

'Okey doke, but don't stay out long. You do have schoolwork, you know.'

'I'll be back in time for lunch.'

Eleven

The Bell Man

I waited until Nan had turned the corner of the lane and was out of sight, then followed Martha into the woods. I guessed she'd gone back to her camp. There was no one else around, and I soon got to the fallen tree covered in ivy. I ducked underneath and went into the secret part of the woods. She couldn't have gone far; there was no way she'd have crossed all the way over to the island in this time. I called her name.

Martha came out from where she had been hiding behind a tree. She looked petrified.

'Really, it's totally cool. I'm not going to dob you in.'

'I do not understand all your words.'

'Well, you talk a bit weird too, if you don't mind me saying. It's all very weird, in fact. I mean, just look at what you're wearing for starters!'

'Your clothes look strange to me too. The way you talk,

the words you use. I have no idea where I am or what is going on.'

We stood there for a minute, looking at each other. Martha was wearing a long, brown skirt made of some rough material, with more skirts underneath and some sort of woolly leggings. She had a tightly fitting jacket of some kind and a shirt underneath that was gathered across her chest. On her feet, there were wooden-soled shoes with leather tops. This was like the costumes we'd looked at when we had a history trip to Hexham gaol. We'd been allowed to try them on, they were dead uncomfortable. But there it was. History. A museum. Was this girl in some sort of historical re-enactment thing?

Martha started to cry. She looked so scared.

Despite the fact she was minging, I went to give her a hug, but then stepped back. Hugging was out, not just because of Covid, but she really did smell bad. Instead, I touched her elbow.

'Don't cry. You can trust me, really you can. Let's go and sit down by the river.'

We walked along the path for a bit, in the gloom of pine trees, her footsteps heavy, dragging. Despite her head being down, she stumbled over tree roots. We walked on, ducking under a fallen tree, then came to a clearing where there was a sandy bank and a shallow stream rushed by. This was where the river splits to go around the island. I used to call it 'the beach' when I came here as a kid with my bucket and spade. We sat down with our legs stretched out in front of us, hers with grubby tights and her wooden shoes, mine in Lycra leggings, stripy socks and walking boots. She pulled her skirt down to cover her legs. We made a right odd pair.

We were quiet for a while, the only sound the rushing of water as the stream rushed over the stones, bright green water plants like streamers danced in the water. We watched as two ducks swam past, not the same as the mallards on the burn: one was white with a black head, the other grey, with a brown head. I wondered what they were and took a photo of them on my phone. I'd ask Grandad when I got back. Turning to Martha, who had gone very quiet, I asked, 'So, you've already told me you're on the run. Do you want to tell me more of what happened?'

'As I said, they took my mother. She told me to run.'

'Who took your mother?'

'The town sheriffs. The Bell Man called for those who suspected their neighbours of witchcraft to come forward. There was a witchfinder in town.'

'Whoa! Hang on. Who or what is the Bell Man first, and second? A *witchfinder*?'

'Every town has a Bell Man. He tells the news. You know, rings the bell and stands in the square and shouts.'

'No, I don't know. I get news from social media.'

'Social…'

'Social media, you know, Instagram, Snapchat, TikTok. Nan has Facebook, and so does my mam, but that's more for oldies.'

I'd clearly lost her. She looked at me with a dazed expression, and I was still none the wiser. It sounded well heavy, though.

'Let's get back to this "Bell Man", I said.

'His words still ring in my ear: "All people that would bring in any complaint against any woman for a witch, they should be sent for and tried by the person appointed."'

'So, I get that the Bell Man reads the news, but who is the witchfinder?'

Martha looked at me, a puzzled expression on her face. 'The witchfinder is the one who hunts out those who are suspected of being a witch. He is the one who will search for the Devil's mark, proof that a woman is a witch.'

'Witchcraft? The Devil? Martha, what year is it?'

'1649.'

'No, it isn't. It's 2020.'

What the actual…? This was bonkers. Was Martha not only lost in place but lost in time too? It might explain her old-fashioned clothes, her tatty hair and rotten teeth and the fear that she had in her eyes. My head was buzzing. I needed to know more. She just looked dazed.

'Tell me more about the witchfinder, Martha. Tell me more about your mother. Is she really a witch?'

'My mother makes cures and charms, heals the sick, but she is no witch. She is kind, God-fearing, a good woman.'

Martha fiddled with the grasses by the bank, tugging at them as she spoke. Her voice, trembling at first, found strength as she continued her story. It was like being in a Netflix film.

'There are plenty who wag their tongues about us, do not approve of our lives, hate my mother. But she is no witch. Goody Pearson, it is she who went to the Bell Man, tugging at his coat, pointing her gnarly fingers at my mother.'

'What a bitch.'

'They came one morning, braying on the door fair fit to knock it down. They dragged my mother from our bed, her kicking, screeching. It was awful. As they dragged her through the door, she told me to run. With our straw pallet still warm from where her body had been I grabbed a few things, tied them in a bundle and fled. I had no idea where to go. To the east was the sea, so I went west. I followed the setting sun on the evening and walked besides the big river, sleeping by its banks, hiding amongst the trees. The river has been good to me. It has given me food and shelter and has kept me hidden.'

'But that doesn't explain how you came to be in 2020 when you left town in 1649.'

'I have no idea,' Martha said. 'I was picking rushes to make a mat to lie on by a narrow wooden bridge that spanned the river. It started raining, so I took shelter underneath. Something caught my eye. There was a flash of silver on the opposite bank, a bright light for a second, then it was gone. When I went up onto the bridge, a hare was running along it over to the other side, so I followed.'

'That's odd, I keep seeing silver flashes too. I saw one yesterday, and when I went to see where it had gone, there were silver threads caught on the bush it had run under.'

'I wished I'd had a snare. I haven't tasted meat in a very long time. The hare was slow, and I thought I might be able to corner it, throw a sack over it. I tried to tread as lightly and carefully as I could. I took off my pattens in case the wooden soles made a noise on the slats of the bridge. I was so preoccupied with the hare that I didn't notice the bridge had changed. The wooden struts had changed into metal. It was the cold of them, sharp through the holes in my woollen hose, that first drew my attention. The hare was gone, and I stood up and looked around. The skies were no longer grey but blue and the sun was shining. There was warmth in the air. The small wooden bridge had grown into a sturdy, metal bridge that was painted green. I had to grip onto the handrail for support, compose myself for a while. Then the bridge clanked, and I could feel vibrations through its base. A man in a red jerkin and with a dog on a rope appeared at the other end. I scurried into the woods and hid.'

'Blimey! Sounds like you've found a portal and stepped through to another time. I've been reading *His Dark Materials* and Will steps through into other worlds using a knife.'

'I have been so afraid.'

'I'm surprised no one has spotted you. There are loads of dogwalkers that come through here. We saw the smoke from your fire the other day. That was when I found your moon. You must have dropped it.'

Martha pulled back her sleeve to reveal the crescent moon, tied around her wrist with dirty red thread. 'This is my mother's amulet – it brings good fortune and protects those who wear it from evil. My mother tore it from her wrist and tossed it to me as she was dragged off.'

Martha started to cry again. 'I think she's in the castle keep. That's where they take those accused of being a witch. Through the black gate. It's an awful place. You can smell the stench of it from the street. I cannot bear the thought of my mother there. She's not done anything wrong.'

We heard voices coming through the woods, and even though we were at the bottom, where hardly anyone came, I thought it better to nip over to the island. No one ever went there.

'Let's hide,' I said.

We crossed the water quickly; it was only shallow. There had been no rain for days. Martha led me on to her camp. As I followed her, my mind was working overtime. I know it feels a bit old-fashioned here at times, but 1649? That's over three hundred years and is one hell of a time warp. What if my friends could see me now! Nothing this exciting happened in town.

At the camp, Martha knelt on the ground and blew on the ashes of her fire, adding some dried grass and thin twigs. Flames appeared, and she added some wood. She put a blackened pan on the fire, balanced on rocks around the flames. She was resourceful, I'd give her that.

'Did you bring that saucepan with you?' I asked.

'No, I found it.' Martha blushed. *Pinched it, more like*, I thought.

'So, are you saying, this Goody Pearson dobbed your mother in. What had she done?'

'I don't know your word "dobbed". Sometimes it is enough to be different. We live on the edge, outsiders. My mother has a tough life, finds it hard to make ends meet. It is not easy when there is no man in the house.'

Martha stirred the pot, then sat back down. 'My mother was a widow and had refused to remarry.'

'Well, that's not a crime, is it?' I thought of my mother, a single parent too.

'There are many who think it so. It is not respectable in the eyes of the Church to live as a single woman.'

'But how?'

'It is enough to be female and untamed, and my mother was wild in their eyes. She refused to dress in plain

112

colours, wore her hair down and walked the streets at night. She did not conform to the teachings of the Church, or to that toad of a man who preached from the pulpit.'

The pot on the fire was simmering now. Martha tore up some wild garlic leaves, adding them to the pot and stirred it before taking it off the flames. She handed me a wooden bowl, the liquid inside rippling as her hands trembled.

'It's not much, but you are welcome to some potage. Before you ask, I did bring this bowl with me. My father made it.'

'Thank you.' It should have been me bringing her food. I was so upset what with Grandad being poorly that I'd totally forgotten I was going to bring her some food and a blanket.

I took it, not wanting to be rude, and looked around for a spoon. There didn't appear to be one, so I brought the bowl up to my lips and took a tentative sip. Bits of green from wild garlic leaves and chunks of potato floated in a murky brown liquid. And I thought my nan's food was bad! It wasn't as bad as it looked, but it wasn't that great, either. I passed the bowl back to her. Probably not a good thing to be doing Covid-wise, but nothing made sense anymore. I felt suspended in a different time and place to the rest of the world altogether over on this island with this girl from the seventeenth century.

'My mam brings me up herself too. Mine got divorced, I'm not sure why exactly. They argued loads and there was a lot of shouting. Dad lives over in Ireland now, back with Nanny McFlynn. She's my dad's mam. We FaceTime each other now, but I guess you don't know what FaceTime is.' Of course she wouldn't know about FaceTime. I was talking too much. I did that when I was nervous or excited. So I asked her, 'What happened to your dad then?'

Martha took a sip of potage then rested the bowl on her lap and looked into the fire. 'I never knew my father. He died of the plague when I was very young. It tore through the town, especially along the Quayside where we lived. They say it came in on the ships. My father was a dockhand. My mother and I were spared, but my father died. That was when the gossip started. They say my mother was spared because she was a witch, and I as her daughter must carry the witch's mark too. But it is her cunning ways, her knowledge of plants and herbs, that keeps us safe. My mother teaches me the ways of her mother and her mother before her. She is very skilled in healing.'

'What was your mother's name?'

'Ann, Ann Watson.'

I'd heard that name before, but where?

Twelve

Grandad

Martha jumped out of her skin when my phone rang, dropping the bowl of potage that had gone cold in her lap. It was my mam. If she had come from the seventeenth century, then I guessed a mobile phone was one step too far for Martha.

'It's only my phone, it's OK, it's my mam.'

Martha's eyes widened and she got up and backed away, staring at my phone.

'Hang on a minute, Mam.' I put my hand over the mouthpiece and whispered to Martha, 'I'll come back tomorrow, bring some more food. You stay out of sight. OK?'

Martha nodded.

I didn't have time to explain the technology of mobiles; I wanted to talk to Mam, so I whispered my goodbyes and left her there, standing by the fire.

'Who was that you were talking to?' Mam said.

'Oh, just this girl I met in the woods. She's… er… walking her dog, the same as me.'

'That's nice, but make sure you stick to social distancing, won't you?'

We'd skip the bit about bowl-sharing and her being from the seventeenth century on the run from the witchfinder then!

'How are you, Mam?'

'Oh, Molly, I'm exhausted. This is a living hell. We've got no PPE, the wards are full, staff catching Covid left, right and centre, and I have never had to deal with so much death and despair.'

'Sounds hideous.'

'Oh, I'm sorry, I didn't mean to blurt all that out. It's hard having no one to offload to when I get home. How's things going with you? I'm sorry I haven't had much time to talk.'

We talked as I walked back to Nan and Grandad's house, and I told her about the trip to Tesco, about Nan weeing behind a bush, which Mam laughed about and said that some things never changed. I told her about the plans for my birthday the next day. Nan had said it was the full moon, and we were going to have a full moon party.

'She thinks she's still on a beach in Goa,' Mam joked. 'Your nan and grandad spent a year in India, doing yoga and partying with the other hippies on the beach. Can't you just see them, floating along the sand in sarongs and sandals, then doing all that tribal drumming stuff as the sun sets?'

Yes, I could, and we had a right laugh imagining them with their tribe of stoned hippies.

This was a different mam to the one I'd said goodbye to a few days ago, tetchy, uptight and glad to see the back of me. It was good to hear her voice. It was good to hear her laugh.

'Grandad isn't very well, though. He's coughing loads and I think he has a temperature.'

Mam's tone of voice changed. She went into nurse mode. 'How high is his temperature? Has he gone for a PCR test?'

'His head was all sweaty, and he looks a horrible colour, and he hasn't gone for a test. He's insisting on finishing something in his workshop. I think it's for my birthday.'

'Right, I'll ring them now. You get back, but make sure you keep well away from him. Do you understand? If he had Covid it is highly contagious. Great! This is all I need!'

Then she was gone. No 'goodbye Molly', no 'Happy Birthday for tomorrow'. I'd put Grandad to the back of my mind while I was talking to Martha about the Bell Man and the witchfinder, but now I had a sick feeling in my stomach. After talking to Mam, I was really worried about Grandad. Or maybe it was the potage! I hurried home.

*

I could hear that Nan was on the phone when I went in, and I guessed she was talking to Mam. She was shouting.

'Did I ask you for your advice? Do you not think I am quite capable of looking after my husband myself?'

117

I stood in the doorway, listening. I could hear my mother's voice, shouting back through the phone.

'Yes, of course I realise it's serious,' Nan said. 'You are not the only one who knows about medicine and disease, you know.'

With that, Nan banged the phone down and swore. I would have to tread carefully, but Mam did have a point. This was serious. If he did have Covid, then he should get tested and isolate.

I picked up my phone and looked for the NHS Covid app. It looked easy to use, so I bypassed Nan, who was muttering to herself and banging saucepans in the kitchen, and went to find Grandad. He was in his usual place in the workshop, sat in his chair by the log burner. He was awake but was just sat there, staring at the floor, not doing anything. I stood in the doorway and made sure I could breathe fresh air while I spoke to him.

'Grandad,' I said softly. He didn't hear, so I tried again, a bit louder: 'Grandad!'

'Ah, Molly, there you are.' He looked up with bleary eyes and started coughing as soon as he spoke.

'Grandad, I think you should go and get tested. You might have Covid. Look, it's easy to book a test on your phone. You just download the Covid app. I can do it for you if you like?'

'Oh, Molly, sounds like a bit of a fuss to me. I've just got a cough. I'll be right as rain soon. Your nan is looking after me. She's brewing up a special concoction, she says, and I hear you went out with her getting coltsfoot today. That'll soon fettle me, lass. Don't you fret. Besides, there's too much to do here to have me gadding about like that.

The potatoes won't get themselves into the ground, and the greenhouse won't water itself.'

'No, Grandad, you need to get tested. If it is coronavirus, then you might pass it on to me or to Nan. You wouldn't want that now, would you? I can water the greenhouse for you, and if you tell me what to do, I'll have a go at planting potatoes, but now we need to get you booked in for a test.'

Grandad sighed. 'You're a good girl, Molly.' Then he slid his phone across the floor to me. After giving me his passcode, I put the app on his phone and booked him in for a drive-through test. The nearest was Carlisle Airport.

'That's miles away!' he said. It was, and it was bonkers there weren't any nearer, but I'd already messaged Mam and promised her I'd make him go for a test. I thought it would easier to get him to book one than argue the toss with Nan. He now had a test booked for 4pm. I went into the house to wash my hands after using his phone. Nan was at her workbench with her back to the door, grinding something in her big pestle and mortar. I stood at the top of the steps and called down to her, 'I've booked Grandad in for a Covid test. Mam thought we should, and so do I.'

I was ready for a fight, but none came. 'Aha,' was all she said without turning around.

Half an hour later and Grandad was heaving himself up and into the van.

'Are you sure you'll be OK driving yourself?' I called.

'No choice, have I, if I'm so darned infectious?'

He banged the door shut and started the engine. I waved from the garden gate and watched the van disappear down the lane. I stood there until it went over the hill and disappeared. Apart from the sound of the water in the burn, it was silent. I hoped desperately he'd be OK. I checked the time on my phone. He'd be a couple of hours.

*

Nan was in her workshop, sat at the table, writing in her book. I pulled up a chair and sat opposite her. I hesitated before I spoke, but took a big breath in and said, 'Mam thinks we should make Grandad isolate, at least until we know one way or another.'

'Oh yes, your mother has been more than generous with her advice,' Nan said, looking up, a bitter expression on her face.

'Nan, she is a nurse on the Covid ward. It's not like she doesn't know what she's talking about. And anyway, you're always moaning about his snoring. You'll get a good night's sleep for once!'

I didn't mention that it was her I could hear through the bedroom wall at night. 'Come on, I'll give you a hand. We can make up a room in the attic.'

Nan huffed a big sigh, muttered something under her breath then banged her pencil down. She leant both hands on the table and stood up with a groan. Nan and Grandad always made old people noises when they got up and down. 'Sounds of the sixties,' Grandad would joke. She followed me up, her feet heavy on the stairs, huffing and puffing as she went.

Nan and Grandad's house had a third floor. There were two rooms and a bathroom up there. They didn't really use it, and although it was full of all kinds of junk, it would be the ideal place for Grandad to self-isolate. In the bigger of the two rooms, there was a bed settee somewhere under all the boxes and bags that had been dumped on it. An exercise bike in the corner was gathering dust and there were boxes of pictures, bags of knitting wool, old toys and piles of books. The roof sloped above us, with three large Velux windows. I stood on a box to open one and looked out. You could see the whole of the garden from up here, and beyond to the fields and then the Tyne. On the opposite side of the river, in the distance, there were hills. You could see the 'spike', a long column of rock up on a hilltop that we all used to walk to with Mam and Dad. A Bronze Age fort, Grandad had told us. Nan and Grandad used to go up there on the Summer Solstice to watch the sun come up. I guessed Nan's knees wouldn't make the climb these days.

I left the window open to let some fresh air in and the dust out, and started shifting the boxes. There was a box of photographs, and on the top one of a small boy, with a woman who I presumed to be his mother.

'Who's this?' I asked.

'Why, that's Joe, your grandad, when he was a lad, and that woman with him was his nanny.'

'She looks far too young,' I said.

'No, not nanny as in Nan, but nanny as in nursemaid. His parents were posh, and he had a nanny who looked after him before he went to boarding school.'

'When did he go to boarding school?'

'When he was seven. He hated it and always said he'd never send his children away.'

'That sounds awful.' I looked again at the photo of the little boy, his hair parted on one side, a toy train in his hand, smart clothes and polished shoes. It almost looked as if he were standing to attention. I felt so sorry for him. He looked sad and scared.

'Joe's family is everything to him,' Nan said. 'He might not have known a loving family himself, but he was darn sure he was going to be the best dad and grandad he could be.'

Poor Grandad! And now he was on his own, driving to Carlisle, no doubt feeling dreadful, facing the prospect of not only being ill but having to isolate at the top of the house, away from his precious garden and workshop. I spent the next hour working as hard as I could, making up his room. I found a box of old gardening magazines, several jigsaws and dusted off some books which I put on a cupboard next to his bed. There were photos in frames too, of Mam with Uncle Andrew and Uncle Paul and of me as a baby, which I cleaned and put on the shelf opposite his bed. We put a radio up there, and his phone charger.

Nan, meanwhile, had come up with a diffuser that puffed out aromatherapy oils and placed a bottle of coltsfoot cough syrup by his bed. She put a few drops of tea tree oil in the diffuser, then disappeared again. She said the tea tree oil would purify the air, and she was away to her workshop to make him some medicine. When I went down, the door to her workshop was firmly shut. I could hear her talking to herself, and I thought I'd leave her to it.

I'd have to get on with some schoolwork at some point, but time was getting on, Grandad would be back at any minute and Nan didn't seem to have thought about getting any tea ready. I opened the fridge to see what I could find to cook.

I found some mince and prepared my signature dish of spaghetti Bolognese. While it was bubbling, I went out to water the greenhouse. It was warm in there and smelt earthy. All around the edge were shelves with little pots of seedlings. I looked at the labels, handwritten on cut-up pieces of plastic: chillies, peppers, aubergines, tomatoes, lettuce, beetroot and watered them gently with the watering can, filling it up from the barrels outside.

I was just putting the spaghetti in a pan of boiling water when I saw the van pull up. It took Grandad a while to get out and I watched him put his head down on his hands on the steering wheel before he did. He looked completely wrung out.

'Keep away, Molly,' he said as he came through the door. His shoulders were hunched, his head down, and he moved as if every bone in his body hurt. 'I'm off to bed.'

'Nan and I have made you a bed upstairs in the top room. I hope you like it. Everyone thinks it's for the best.'

Grandad nodded, then grabbed the handrail with a trembling hand and plodded slowly up the stairs. I had a big lump in my throat.

'I'll bring up your tea and leave it on the landing,' I called up after him. 'I've made spaghetti Bolognese,' but there was no response.

I wore a mask when I took up Grandad's tea and left it on a tray outside his door. Until his test results were back, I was taking no chances. Nan said she was too busy and would have hers later, so I sat by myself at the table. It was my birthday tomorrow. I checked my phone for messages. There was one from Mam asking if Grandad had got tested, but none from my so-called friends. *Thanks, guys, I miss you too!*

Thirteen

Birthday Girl

My dad FaceTimed me! It was so good to see him even if it was only seven o'clock in the morning and he'd woken me up. Nanny McFlynn was there too, although you could only see the top half of her head on the screen. They were singing 'Happy Birthday' and Dad was playing his guitar. Even their dog was joining in! They were hilarious. Dad's hair was getting long and grey, his curls bouncing on his shoulders as he played. I couldn't wait until I could go across to Ireland and stay with them, though with the pandemic, goodness knows when that would be.

Mam hadn't totally forgotten either. She sent me a message, wishing me Happy Birthday and saying she'd ring later. I guessed she was at work. She said her present was in the post. Dom from drama club video-called me too – like me, he was still in bed. He was surrounded by a rainbow of pillows. He's lush, he is. He said he was sick of being in his

124

bedroom, and there was nothing to get up for. Poor Dom. He looked right fed up. It was still early so I wasn't surprised that Jess or Shona or Abby hadn't messaged. I wasn't going to waste any time thinking about them, though. I could hear Nan singing in the kitchen below and the smell of a cake being baked was wafting up the stairs, so I jumped out of bed, grabbed my dressing gown and ran down.

'Happy Birthday!' Nan shouted. There were jugs of daffodils on the table and a big chocolate cake on a glass cake stand in the middle. She looked like summer sunshine itself, dressed in lime green and pink, and surrounded by bright yellow flowers.

'When did you make that?' I asked, looking at the most splendid chocolate cake I had ever seen. Nan had been in her workshop mixing potions for Grandad when I went to bed last night. It was three layers tall, and covered in buttercream icing, with little purple flowers on the top.

'Oh, who needs sleep? I certainly don't! Come on, open your presents.'

There were three presents on the table.

The first was a smooth, round wooden box with a fitted lid. It was beautiful. The grain of the wood flowed in bands around it. It felt wonderful in my hands, and I put it up to my nose to smell it.

'It's cherry wood,' Nan said, 'from the tree in the garden. He thought you could put your rings and earrings in it.' It was perfect, and I loved that Grandad had made it himself.

I rushed up to the landing and stood at the bottom of the stairs that led to the attic. 'Thank you, Grandad! It's wonderful! You're so clever! I love you!'

He tried to call back down, but he coughed and spluttered with every word.

'Don't talk! I'll bring you some cake!' I clattered back down the stairs and sat at the table. My phone pinged. It was Grandad. He was using WhatsApp.

Glad you like it. Happy birthday, Molly xxx

I snapped a selfie of me holding the box and sent it straight back:

you're the best! thank you 😍

'Now, these are from me,' Nan said, handing me two presents, both wrapped in wrinkled paper. Nan always unwrapped presents carefully, snipping the Sellotape with little scissors so it didn't rip the paper, then smoothing it out and folding it so it could be used again. The first present was heavy, hard. It was a lump of pale pink crystal.

'Rose quartz, the crystal of unconditional love.'

'It's beautiful, thank you,' I said, holding it up to the light.

'And so are you, Molly,' Nan said, stroking my face and tucking a strand of hair behind my ear. 'I hope you will learn to love yourself, just the way you are, and know that you are very loved in return.'

I swallowed hard. My emotions were all over the place. It was so hard being me. I hated the way I looked, the size I was. The constant battle to lose weight. How unpopular I was, the stupid mistakes I'd made, how hard I found it to make friends.

126

'Come on, open your other present!' Nan said, putting a book-shaped present in my hands. I unpeeled the wrapping carefully. It was a hard-backed notebook with a beautiful picture of a hare and the moon on the front and blank pages inside.

'I thought you could do some drawing or keep a journal. I find writing down my feelings help me sort them out in my head.'

I got up and flung my arms around Nan. 'Thank you! You are the best.' I really meant that. After yesterday's chat and Nan offloading all that stuff about herself, I felt I'd gained a friend as well as getting to know a grandparent again.

'I know you miss your life in town, Molly, and I'm sorry you are disappointed not to be going out with your friends, but I'm rather glad there has been this lockdown and you are here. Selfish of me, I know.'

'You know what, I'm kind of glad too.'

'We'll have fun tonight, just the two of us, under the pink full moon. Our very own full moon party! Now, let's have cake for breakfast!'

It was in no shape or form what I had planned with my friends, but it was better than nothing. I only hoped she wasn't going to go playing the bongos or dancing naked in the moonlight!

I laughed. 'Yes, let's!' Nan cut two slices of cake and poured herself some coffee from their ancient coffee pot on the Rayburn. Cake for breakfast! She was the best.

The cake was wonderful, rich and chocolatey. Meg sat right next to me, dribble landing in spots on the stone floor. She looked hopeful. There was no way.

Nan made a tray up for Grandad and said she was going up to check on him. She'd made him some medicine which she poured into a cup with some hot water. It looked brown and turgid and smelt awful.

'What's in that?' I asked, wrinkling up my nose.

'Well, it's a concoction of echinacea root, elderberry for boosting immunity, elecampane root, angelica for strengthening and protecting, birch polypore to give anti-inflammatory support, and turkey tail fungus.'

'And I suppose you mixed it up in your cauldron?' I laughed.

'Don't mock me, Molly. This is powerful medicine. I'm sure Joe just has a bit of flu or a nasty cold, but to be on the safe side, I'm giving him this. It'll boost his immune system if nothing else. While we're at it, we'll take some ourselves. Prevention is better than cure, as they say!'

'Do I have to? It looks disgusting.'

Nan was already pouring it into a shot glass. She added a bit of hot water to it from the kettle. 'Down in one! We'll pretend it's tequila, eh? Cheers!' Nan said, and necked it. She'd clearly done shots before.

'Nan, you should wear a mask, and so should Grandad,' I said, as she picked up his tray, 'and gloves.'

'Oh, I'll be alright,' she said. 'Strong as an ox, me. I'll keep my distance, though, don't worry.'

But I did worry. I was worried about Grandad, and about Nan. I was also worried about Martha and Mam. While Nan was upstairs, I cut another sliver of cake, stuffed it in my mouth, then cut a bigger piece, wrapped it in clingfilm, left a note, grabbed Meg's lead and headed out the door.

Fourteen

The Gathering

With Meg running circles around me, still hopeful of getting cake, I headed down the lane. There was the hare again, sat in a gateway, the morning sun shining behind it. I paused, watched it for a minute, and it stared straight back at me, before running across the field. I watched it go, shielding my eyes from the bright light. I don't remember seeing this many brown hares when I used to come here as a kid.

All the way down the lane, daffodils had come out and were nodding in the breeze. It looked pretty. I noticed the white blossom of the sloe bushes, and the bright green leaves on the hawthorn and new-born lambs in the fields. They looked so cute. I paused by a gateway and watched them running in groups, like gangs from a youth club, up and down the fields. They sprang from all four feet, up in the air, twisting, turning. Two birds with long curved beaks were swirling around just about the grass, making kind of bubbling noises. I'd downloaded a neat app – BirdNET. It lets you record birdsong and then tells you what the bird is. The app told me they were curlews. I smiled. Despite Grandad being poorly, this was turning into an alright birthday.

Someone had been painting stones. There were five of them, in a line, spaced out along the side of the path on the way into the woods. Rainbows, hearts and the NHS logo were painted with bright colours. *What a nice thing to do*, I thought.

I dodged the dogwalkers and, when no one was looking, ducked under the fallen tree, slipped over the stream and went on to the island.

'I've brought you some birthday cake,' I called, as I approached Martha's camp, then instantly thought how stupid I'd been. This was the second time I'd turned up without any proper food. I should have brought some bread or cheese or something a bit more nutritious. I put the cake wrapped in clingfilm down on a log at the camp then I stepped back as Martha came out from her shelter, careful to keep my distance.

Martha looked at it as if she'd never seen a slice of cake before, then went to put it in her mouth.

'Don't eat the clingfilm!' I unwrapped it for her and handed it back, licking my fingers.

She took a bite and winced. 'Don't you like chocolate cake?'

'It hurts my teeth. It is so sweet.' This didn't seem to put her off, as she stuffed the rest of the cake in, laughing as she did it. Chocolate dribble fell from her mouth and onto her top.

'I don't want to be rude, but you could do with a trip to a dentist.'

'Dentist? Birthday?'

'You don't get presents on your birthday?'

'I do not know the exact year of my birth or the date. My mother tells me it was around midsummer, and I think I am fifteen but cannot be sure.'

I sat on the ground. 'Can I ask you a favour?'

'Me?' Martha said. 'How can I help you?'

'You know you said your dad had the plague. Can I ask how you and your mother kept yourselves healthy and how she treated others who were sick?'

'I was very small when the pestilence took my father, but I have watched my mother and helped her gather herbs and make potions and balms ever since. She wrote many of her recipes in her book. I have it with me. It was her mother's before her, and her most precious possession. I was careful to fetch it from the house after she was taken.'

Martha reached into a cloth bag that was hidden underneath some branches and brought out a book with a brown leather cover. It had a crescent moon on the front. Despite the warmth of the day, I got goosebumps and the hairs on my arm stood on end.

*

When I held the book, it was like there was an electric current running through my fingers and up my arms. I didn't know how or why, but I felt it, deep inside, a fluttering in my belly. Bits of paper and cloth were stuck over pages of writing and drawings, some flying loose in the breeze as Martha opened it. It wasn't the same book as Nan's, but the format was the same: drawings of plants and flowers, and notes, symbols, rhymes and recipes.

'My mother calls this a Gathering,' Martha said, as she handed me the book. 'It was my grandmother's, and she passed it down to my mother.'

I ran my fingers over the pages, lifting the loose pieces, some as delicate as a butterfly's wing. Tears pricked in the corner of my eyes.

I passed it back to Martha. 'My nan has a book just like this.'

Martha held the Gathering to her chest and rocked backwards and forwards, her eyes closed.

After a while, I took a deep breath and spoke. 'My grandad is sick. I'm scared he's got coronavirus.'

Martha opened her eyes and looked at me. It seemed as if all the energy had drained out of her, as if the book was opening a wound made when her mother was taken. Her voice was thin, barely audible. 'Corona…?'

'Coronavirus – it's this pandemic that the whole world has got. It started in Wuhan in China. It's killing millions of people, and there are no cures or vaccines for it, yet.'

'It sounds like the Pestilence. So many were lost to that, my father included.' Martha put her hand across her heart and looked up to the sky.

'Yes, so you said, and I'm sorry about your dad, but can you have a look and see if there is anything in your book that might help my grandad?' I instantly regretted being so snappy when I saw Martha's eyes widen and her head go down to the Gathering.

'First, you must protect yourselves,' said Martha, thumbing through the book. 'My mother uses Four Thieves Vinegar to wash our hands and face before venturing out and upon return. We use it whenever we are called to the sick.'

'Ah, it's OK, we have anti-bac hand gel and masks these days. I think we've moved on from vinegar!'

Martha looked a bit offended, so I backtracked a bit. 'So, what's in this Four Thieves Vinegar then?'

Martha put the Gathering on my lap, open at a page. On it were drawings of lots of flowers and herbs, and writing underneath, but I couldn't decipher the text.

'You'll have to read it out, I'm sorry,' I said.

'Do you not know your letters? My mother taught me to read. She could read too. That was another reason for folk to cast suspicion on us.'

'Never! So, it wasn't OK to be single, and it wasn't OK to read? That's heavy.'

Martha pointed with her finger at the different drawings, and said the names out loud: 'Angelica, camphor, cloves, garlic…'

'Hang on a minute, I'll make a note of these in my phone, and take some photos so I can recognise them. OK, carry on.'

'…marjoram, meadowsweet, wormwood and sage. Make a brew with vinegar and dab on hands and face before going out.' She looked up and said, 'It's really good for killing fleas, too.'

We'd learnt about the plague in history and how it was carried by fleas on rats. *So, was the plague a virus, just like Covid?* I wondered. Had Martha stumbled into our times for a reason? Had she knowledge that would help? I listened more carefully to the words Martha was reading. They were strange, yet somehow familiar, like I'd heard them before. Her voice was frail, but those words, weaving through the sounds of birdsong and running water, had a kind of strength. It occurred to me that this was actually really cool and something quite powerful was at play. I couldn't believe I was sitting here talking about herbs and flowers to a girl who lived in plague times and looked like she had come from the pages of a history book, whose mother was in prison accused of witchcraft and who had time-travelled through a portal under the bridge. A couple of days ago I was gutted not to be going out in town, choosing my Pandora ring, getting a bellybutton piercing and going to Wagamama with my mates for my birthday.

Martha was still reading from the Gathering: 'Wash the walls and burn the clothes your grandfather has been wearing. Fires will also purge the pestilence, and the ringing of bells.'

I had my doubts about the bell bit, but the other stuff all seemed worth a try, and Grandad's clothes could always do with a good hot wash.

'My mam is a healer of sorts too, she's a nurse. Works at the hospital. She used to be a midwife, but she's on the Covid ward now, which I guess would be like a plague ward. She's completely exhausted. There are thousands of people dying. She said the other night that the bodies were piling up in the morgue.'

'The bodies piled up in the street the last time the Pestilence visited. I was only small, but I do remember the smell. My mother made good coin selling nosegays.'

'What's a nosegay?' I asked – not that we had bodies piling up in the street.

'Anything that smells fresh: violets, lavender, sweet marjoram. It is, after all, the smell that carries the disease.'

'No, it isn't! It's a virus, it is airborne, but you can't catch it from a smell.'

'This word, virus, is new to me.'

'I guess it's the same thing as your pestilence, except viruses weren't known about then. They're still not that sure what to do about them, even now.'

'The Pestilence brings a terrible death.' Martha had looked back at her mother's book, and began reading: 'First comes the fever, with coughing and pains in the chest.'

She looked up at me. 'Does your grandad cough much?'

'Yeah, he can hardly talk for coughing.'

Martha bit her lip then ran her fingers along the page. 'Then the swellings appear, the skin turns black and the sick stagger as if drunk.'

'He's not got any swellings as far as I know.'

She continued reading: 'Death comes swiftly within a few days.'

'That's enough!' I didn't want to hear any more.

Martha looked at me and carried on: 'The Church says it is divine punishment for the sins of the town. There was also a full eclipse of the moon just before the Pestilence hit Newcastle. It was a bad omen. Has there been an eclipse of late in your time?'

I couldn't bear to think of Grandad dying. I was dreading him getting his results back. It was all I could think about. I snapped at Martha again. 'What a load of tosh! I've got no idea about an eclipse. It's a virus, and it's come from Wuhan in China, and they will find a vaccine and a cure, and in the meantime, between Mam and Nan, you and me, Grandad will get better, he must!'

'You could give him some posset-ale to induce sweating,' Martha said, her voice trembling. I was sorry I'd shouted at her.

She found her place in the book and ran her shaking finger over words and pictures: 'Fennel and marigolds in winter, and sorrel, burglass and borage in summer. Also, wood sorrel, scabious, rosemary, yarrow and butterbur.'

'Butterbur? I know that one! My grandad showed me it when we came down here the other day. It grows down in the sand on the other side of the stream. I'm going to go and get some now! Coming?'

*

I grabbed Martha's hand and pulled her up. I'd forgotten all about social distancing again. Mind you, who had she seen lately? I reckoned she'd be safe. Meg, who had been asleep while we talked, jumped up, excited to be off to the river.

Just as we were about to cross the water to the mainland, we heard dogs barking and a lot of shouting. Meg growled and I grabbed her muzzle to silence her. Men's voices, heavy boots crashing through the woods and the shrill sound of a dog whistle.

I turned to tell Martha to hide, but she'd already disappeared. She didn't need telling. A frightened rabbit doesn't wait to see who's chasing her. I backtracked to the camp and found her crouched in the dark at the very back of her den.

There was no smoke coming from the fire, but I kicked some sand over it just to be on the safe side and quickly covered her shelter with a couple of fallen branches. You couldn't tell it was there unless you really looked hard.

'I can't hear them anymore,' I whispered. 'Stay there, I'll go check the coast is clear.'

Sure enough, the men had gone, but I thought I'd better go on a bit to double-check. I crossed the water and walked down the path that led to the green bridge. I could see them in a line on top of the bridge. Some of them were looking towards the island through binoculars.

There were four of them. I recognised one of them – he was the gamekeeper at the other farm, the one before the village. Nasty piece of work, my nan said. As I approached, I recognised the son from up at the farm, Matt. He used to tease me when I came to stay with Nan and Grandad as a kid: 'townie', he called me. I used to have a crush on him, couldn't think why now. There was nothing but contempt in his face, his top lip snarling, full of bravado. All four were dressed in tweedy green and brown clothes, like cow shit, I thought. The gamekeeper had a gun cocked over his arm. My heart started thumping as I approached them. I had to do something, distract them somehow.

'Bird-watching, are we?' Cheeky, I know, but it got their attention away from the woods.

'It is the mating season, didn't you know?' the gamekeeper said, licking his lips, and the others all sniggered. He took a swig from a silver hip flask and passed it to the guy next to him.

'I don't see anything remotely attractive,' I said, staring him back in his cold grey eyes.

'You're new round here,' a guy with sandy curls said, looking me up and down, giving me 'that look' that some lads do, talking to my tits and not my face.

'She stays with those hippy freaks at the cottage down from the farm. I'd recognise that tatty mutt anywhere,' Matt said. He poked Meg with a stick on her back legs. She faltered, whimpered and cowered behind my legs.

'Get off my dog, who do you think you are, Matt Thompson?'

The guys drew themselves up to their full heights, puffed out their chests, and even though I was shaking inside, I stood my ground. The gamekeeper put his hands on his hips and came up too close to me for comfort. He lowered himself so his face was in my face. I could smell the whisky on his breath.

'Seen any more dodgy people round here, have you? We've had notice there's a tramp living in the woods.' I stepped back to avoid the spittle that flew from his mouth as he spoke but backed into another of the guys, who shoved me forwards and back into the green woollen chest of the gamekeeper. I could feel tears pricking.

'No, I've been walking my dog down there. I assure you, there's no one there. Now, I'm just going to the shop. Excuse me,' I said, and pushed my way through them. Meg cowered close to the ground as she walked. My legs had turned to jelly. I looked round and they were all watching me, laughing, and one of them started wobbling the sides of the bridge, which made it shake. I walked as fast as I could without breaking into a run, then once I was out of sight and over the other side, I jumped down under the bridge and wiped away hot tears of anger on my sleeve.

I hid amongst some tall rushes, holding Meg close to my side and waited until the coast was clear. I had to get back to Martha. As I crouched there, I looked along the bridge supports – strong metal girders – and thought of Martha's story about following the path of them and coming out in our time. I would have kept to the underside too, but I was on the wrong side of the river, and I didn't fancy swimming, so I waited for a bit. I heard their heavy boots overhead and their talk about going to the pub. When I was sure they'd gone, I legged it across the bridge and into the woods as fast as I could.

'They've gone!' I said. Both Meg and I were panting as I peered into Martha's den. I could see the whites of her eyes in the dark at the back.

'I fear I must go too,' Martha said, coming out. She rushed about, picking things up, dropping them, going round in circles.

'Stop it!' I put my hand on her arm. 'You're going nowhere other than coming back with me.'

'No. I cannot risk being seen.'

'Look, you could do with some light relief and no doubt some food. We're going to have a party tonight for my birthday. It's a full moon party! There's cake! You can stay at our house!'

Fifteen

Pink Moon Rising

Martha refused to leave the woods. I tried everything – tempting her with clean clothes, a shower, cake – then I got annoyed with her. There was only so much I could do. If she wanted to stay put, then so be it. This was my birthday. I'd already had it ruined by lockdown, so I was going to try and salvage what I could of it, even if that meant howling at the moon with my nan.

I sat on the window seat in my bedroom, with my back against the thick, stone wall, my legs stretched out in front of me. This had become my favourite thinking spot. I had Mam's present in my hands, which had been waiting for me when I got in. It had arrived by Special Delivery. I wondered if Mam had remembered we were going shopping for a Pandora ring before lockdown. I wasn't sure if that was what I wanted anymore. It was a small parcel, so I guessed it might be jewellery. I unwrapped it, and sure enough, it was a Pandora ring. It said it was an April birthstone ring, although the leaflet inside said the stone was man-made. I put the ring on and held my hand up in front of me, took a photo and sent it to Mam with a thank-you message. My hands had changed. The black and white acrylics were long gone, and I hadn't bothered doing anything else. I couldn't remember the last time I'd gone so long without doing my nails. They weren't in great shape, and there were rinds of dirt under them. Mam video-called me back.

I got a shock. There were red marks on her face and sores on her nose and chin. Her eyes were bloodshot, her hair greasy and unwashed. She looked like she hadn't slept for a week.

'Mam, you look awful! What are those marks on your face?'

'Happy Birthday, sweetheart,' she said, ignoring my tactless comment. She looked totally wrung out. 'Do you like your ring?' she asked.

'I love it! Look,' and I held up my hand for her to see.

'Ooh, your nails could do with some attention!' Her face screwed up in disapproval.

'Yeah, I've been gardening, sorry!' Trust her to find fault.

'Gardening? You?'

'Yeah, I'm helping Grandad because he's all stressed about getting his veggies planted. It's actually quite fun. I'm going to plant peas tomorrow.'

'How is he?'

'He's not great, Mam, his test results should be through soon. Nan and I made up his bed in the attic, and he's isolating up there, just in case. We're making some herbal remedies for him. I'm learning how to make coltsfoot cough syrup. I've done loads of research. I'm going to make—'

Mam interrupted. 'What's his temperature?'

'I don't know – Nan says he's hot and sweaty, so I guess it's high. We're going to use butterbur to bring down his fever.'

'For crying out loud! Does she still think this is the Middle Ages? Molly, I'll go on Amazon and get an oximeter to measure his oxygen levels, and a thermometer gun. I'll get it delivered there. I'll ring back after 6pm when my shift finishes, and I want to talk to your grandmother. I've got to go now, I'm due at work.'

'Before you go, Mam, what happened to your face?'

'It's from the face masks we wear. They must be tight to try and stop us catching Covid. Mind you, they're no use, and we're running out of clean scrubs all the time. Still, never mind me, I'm fine. I hope you enjoy the rest of your birthday, and I'm only sorry I can't be with you.'

Mam's voice cracked with emotion again, and so did mine as I said goodbye to her. I wanted to say, 'I love you,' but the words wouldn't come.

*

I came downstairs to show Nan my ring and found her crying in the kitchen. She was listening to some right dreary music which was playing on an old-fashioned record player. She was miles away, singing the words but blubbing at the same time. I wrapped my arms around her shoulders.

'Nan! What are you doing to yourself? Is it Grandad? Has he got his results?'

I reached for a wad of tissues and passed them to her. She nodded. 'He's got Covid.' Nan was crying out loud now, big sobs, her shoulders heaving up and down, snot everywhere.

'Oh, Nan. He'll get better. We'll make him better, just you see. Sounds like you are torturing yourself with this music, though. It's dead dreary.'

'It's "Pink Moon" by Nick Drake. It's one of "our tunes". I thought it fitting what with it being the full pink moon but hadn't realised what memories it holds for your grandad and me. He bought it from a record shop in town called Listen Ear, when we were first going out together.'

Nan blew her nose again and, through her tears, said, 'You should have seen your grandad then. He had long henna'd hair which hung in curls from a battered trilby hat. I remember the owner of the record shop shouting, "Oi, hippie! You'll love this!"'

Nan reached for a photo in a frame to show me. He had piercing blue eyes and tanned skin, bare-chested, with a silver chain around his neck and a dangly elephant earring. His mouth was slightly open, his lips full.

'He was good-looking!' I said.

'Yes, he was. Not only was he incredibly handsome, but he was kind and gentle, and loved me just the way I was. After years of one-night stands and being hurt by guys, he was the one who rescued me. He showed me what real love was, and that it was OK to be me.'

No wonder Nan was so upset and worried about

Grandad. He was her rock. We had to get him well. I could tell from how snappy she'd been lately that she was really worried about him. So was I. He'd smoked all his life, as far as I knew, and the virus was all about the lungs. It was supposed to hit older people worse too.

'Nan, you know you're into herbal remedies. I've been, um, learning about herbs too.'

Nan looked up and over the top of her glasses. 'Erm, on the internet! I've been reading up on the plague times, and the herbs they would use then. I found butterbur by the stream if you want me to pick some, it says that's good for fever, and yarrow too.'

'Well, well, well, quite the cunning woman, Molly. I'm impressed. Yarrow isn't growing just yet, but I've got some dried from last year. That's an excellent shout. I'm working on a compound based on my elderberry, elecampane and echinacea blend, but with added anti-viral properties. I was going to go looking for birch polypore in the woods today. I'm sure I saw some on a dead birch when we were there yesterday. I'd love your help. We'd make a powerful force, the two of us.'

'I'm not convinced Mam approves.'

'Modern medicine has its place, Molly, but your mam should realise there's wisdom in the old stuff too. They should go hand in hand, a gathering of knowledge.'

Gathering. There was that word again.

'Speaking of working hand in hand, Mam is sending something to measure Grandad's oxygen levels and temperature. She says they're working on Covid vaccines and anti-viral drugs all the time but to give him paracetamol and ibuprofen.'

'Yes, yes, I'm already giving him that, and vitamin C and zinc. I am glad of her support, and yours too, but there aren't any modern treatments for Covid yet. We must also draw on herbal lore, use the recipes and healing powers that have been our gifts, passed down by the women who have gone before. You have the gift, Molly, I can feel it very strongly.'

Nan gripped my hand, and we looked each other in the eye. We both started welling up, so I changed the subject.

'I'm going to go out to look at the moon, Nan. It's just coming up! I want to get some photos. Are you coming?'

'No, you go. I want to go and check on your grandad, take him some fresh water and run him a bath. I'll come and join you later.'

'You will wear a mask, won't you?'

'Yes, Molly, I will. Then we'll light a fire outside. I'm sorry I'm being such a misery on your birthday!'

*

The moon was just rising above the fields, a huge disc of pink light. I walked a bit further down the lane to get a better photo. These would look amazing on Instagram. Everywhere there was a milky pink light and an eerie silence. Even the lambs had stopped bleating. It was as if the earth was holding its breath as the moon rose. I felt its magnetism, just like Nan had talked about, and as I watched it rise into the sky I stood, arms stretched wide, feeling its power. The hairs on my arms were stood on end, goosebumps all along them.

'Please make Grandad better,' I said out loud.

145

Thank goodness no one could hear me!

Then something caught my eye in the oak tree. It was hard to see with the moon behind it. The strong branches were black against the moon's light, but there was a shape in the middle of the tree. Someone or something was in the bowl in the middle, the place I used to climb up into to sit with Grandad when I was little.

'Is someone there?' I called. There was a shifting sound, and I walked up to the base of the trunk and looked up.

'I am not coming down,' the voice said.

'Martha? Is that you?'

'Yes, but I am not coming down.'

'So, you said! Hang on, I'll come up!'

The rock was still at the base of the tree, where Grandad had put it so I could reach up to the first branch. I stepped on it and stretched up, swinging myself into the tree. From there it was easy to climb up into the bowl where Martha was sat.

'I wanted to come and wish you Happy Birthday. I've made you something,' she said, handing me a stone. It was a flat, round pebble, no doubt smoothed by the river. I held it up in the moonlight. There was a hare painted on one side.

'Wow! This is amazing, Martha. Thank you. How did you make it? Where did you get the paint from?'

'I mixed clay and charcoal from the fire and used a reed to draw.'

'Thank you. It's so special.'

'You are welcome. It was a hare that guided me to you.'

'I remember. I keep seeing hares too. I wonder if it's the same one?'

We sat there for a while, listening to the hoot of an owl and watching the moon change from pink to bright white as it rose high into the black night sky. I reached for Martha's hand and held it. The moonlight lit up the tears that were falling down her cheeks. I guessed she was just like me: when you've held all your emotions inside, the fear, the hurt and when someone is kind to you, you cry.

From the tree I could see down the lane, the farm on top of the hill and Nan and Grandad's house, the light on in the attic bedroom where Grandad was. I sent him one of the moon pictures. In the garden I could see Nan had lit a bonfire, the flames leaping into the darkness. She'd got out her penny whistle and music floated in the air, cheerful and light. We both shivered at the same time.

'Come on,' I said, jumping down from the tree, 'it's time for you to meet my nan.'

Martha stayed put, shivering in the bowl of the tree. 'I cannot.'

'Yes, you can! There's a warm fire, and we've got pizza and marshmallows. Come on! It's just my nan. No men. Besides, I think you should meet her.'

Sixteen

Pink Moon Party

Martha was shaking, and I had to hold her hand and lead her inside. Nan was nowhere to be seen, and with Grandad up in the attic, I smuggled her into the house with no bother.

'Right, first things first. Go and get a shower in there, and I'll sort you some clothes. You're not coming to my party looking like that! Here's a clean towel.'

I handed her a towel and showed her to the bathroom before she had time to protest. She was proper whiffy, and besides, she needed to lose the historic garb. She just stood here, wide-mouthed, looking around.

'Ah, so I guess you won't know how this all works,' I said, turning on the shower.

'It's a miracle,' she said, as hot water and steam came out of the shower head.

'Not really, it's archaic!' I said. 'You should see the new wet room we've got in the flat.'

148

I gave her a shampoo bar and some soap, and said I'd leave her to it, while I went and put her clothes in the washing machine. I reckoned they'd need a couple of washes. I didn't have many spare clothes, but I found her some leggings and gave her a green jumper – another of Nan's creations that I thought might help to keep her hidden. I was sure Nan wouldn't mind. I looked at my Docs and considered giving them to her, but maybe that was a step too far. She could have an old pair of trainers I'd brought with me.

It was a different girl that stood in front of the mirror once she was dried and dressed. Her hair shone, and her skin glowed. She was beautiful. I sat next to her on the window seat and started on the tats in her hair.

'Thank you,' she said, smiling. 'If my mother could see me now.' Then her face fell.

'That's enough, we're not getting maudlin now! Let's go party!'

We clattered down the stairs and went out into the garden, where we found Nan kneeling at the edge of the burn.

'Ah, Molly, I wondered where you'd got to. Help me up, will you?'

I helped her up and picked up a colander of crystals. 'What are you doing?'

'I'm just washing my crystals. Who's this, a new friend?'

'Nan, this is Martha, and Martha, this is my nan, I mean, Sarah.'

Martha didn't say anything; she just stood there, twiddling the crescent moon bracelet on her wrist.

Nan looked at it, then at Martha. 'Cat got your tongue?' Nan said.

'She's just a bit shy,' I said. 'She's new around here.'

Nan looked at her, smiled and, with open arms, said, 'You're very welcome, Martha.'

I wondered if Nan would bombard her with awkward questions, ask about the moon bracelet with the red thread.

'I didn't think you'd mind Martha coming to my party as it was outside. We'll keep our distance.'

Nan just flapped her spare hand, picking up her drink with the other. 'Pshaw!'

She wasn't bothered and went back to her crystals, picking them up one by one and holding them up in the moonlight.

'Clear quartz, bring strength to Joe's lungs,' she said, her voice a little slurred. 'Rose quartz, help free us all from the anxiety this has brought.'

'You'll have to excuse my nan, she's a bit eccentric,' I said to Martha, who was wide-eyed and silent. We went and stood around the fire, leaving Nan to finish arranging her crystals.

'We need some music!' Nan announced, stretching her arms out wide.

'I've got Spotify on my phone. Shall I find those 3 Daft Monkeys again you like?'

'Yes, Molly, do! Turn it up as loud as it will go, and I'll go find some paraffin. I fancy doing some fire-juggling, just like a proper full moon party. Oh, you should have seen Joe and me back in the day. He was amazing with a fire staff.'

It was another of their festival habits. It was something my dad did too, except he did fire-breathing. It used to drive my mam mad. He'd take a mouthful of paraffin then spit it out while holding a flaming torch, making a huge flame. I'd forgotten about all this, but as Nan dipped two balls on the end of chains into a jug of paraffin and then lit them, the memories came flooding back. She held the two chains at arm's length and then started twirling them in time to the music. They made a whooshing noise and flecks of lighted paraffin spun off as they made the most fantastic shapes. When I took a photo, you could see the traces of the circles. It was well cool. Then she bashed them together by mistake and one hit her head.

'Shit!' Nan said.

There was a smell of singed hair and Nan laughed. Martha hadn't moved from the spot and was staring open-mouthed at my nan.

'Oops-a-daisy!'

'Nan, you nearly set fire to yourself.'

'Oh, I'm fine! Needed a haircut anyway! You have a go!'

'Er, no, you're OK, thanks. I think you'd better put them down now.'

'Little Miss Spoil-Sport!'

'Nan, you've been drinking, put them down! Come on, Martha, let's go and get some pizza.'

Martha, of course, had never had pizza before but thought it wonderful. The rest of the evening was a bit of a damp squib. Nan got proper tipsy, banged her drum a bit, and then said she had a headache and was going inside. Martha and I sat around the fire toasting marshmallows on sticks. I showed her how to hold them low down in the fire, toasting them all over by turning the sticks. It was something Grandad had taught me.

'They're hot! Be careful,' I said as Martha winced when she took a bite.

'No, it's like the cake, it hurts my teeth.'

'Those teeth of yours!'

'I must return to the woods now, Molly. This has been quite a night.'

'Oh, come on! Stay over. I'll sleep on the floor; you can have my bed.'

'No, Molly, I am ready to go back now.'

'Well, take some pizza with you!'

'Thank you. I will.'

With that, Martha disappeared into the night. Before I went in, I looked up to the roof at the back of the house where a faint light was coming from the Velux windows. I missed Grandad and sent him a message to say I was thinking about him and hoped he was OK, but he didn't send one back. Perhaps he was asleep. I'll try and FaceTime him tomorrow.

*

Up in my room, with the last slice of chocolate cake and a mug of hot chocolate, I spread my presents out on the bed: Martha's hare stone, Mam's Pandora ring, Grandad's wooden box, and Nan's rose quartz crystal and the notebook. I picked up Grandad's box and felt terrible that he'd been out in the cold workshop finishing it for me when he was so ill. It was beautiful. Running my hands over the smooth surface of the wood, I could feel his love in it. Then an idea came. With Grandad so sick in bed, and all the farmer's markets cancelled, how about me selling his wooden boxes and bowls online? I'd uploaded the photo I'd taken this morning of me with my present, and it had got loads of likes. I could even set him up with his own Instagram account.

It had been a strange birthday. Not the one I had expected, but it had kind of worked. Best of all was Martha coming down out of the woods and waiting for me in the oak tree. I picked up the painted stone and held it in my palm. Martha was a true friend and had shown more friendship by sitting in that tree than any of my so-called friends in town had ever shown. It was always about them, how they looked, the performances they gave. Jess had put a post on her Insta story with a photo of us, added a gif of a stupid party hat and tagged me in it, saying 'Happy Birthday to my bestie', but she was the only one who had remembered, and the whole 'bestie' thing seemed so false. It wouldn't have killed her to get in touch in person, send a message or give me a call to wish me a happy birthday. I was just snuggling down to go to sleep when Dom rang.

'Hey, you! Happy Birthday!'

'Dom! Great to hear from you. Thanks. It's been… weird.'

'How come?'

'Oh, where to start! Nan's gone full hippy on me, twirling fire, banging her drum and cleansing her crystals, and Grandad's laid up in bed with the Rona. Still, I've got cake, and a new friend. I met her in the woods, she's…' I was about to tell Dom all about her, but I didn't know where to start. 'Enough of me, though, how are you, Dom?'

'Oh, just great, not. I was attacked.'

'What?'

'I was walking home from the shops – had just been for a few bits for my mam – when Gareth Swindle and his crew started walking with me, taking the piss, mincing and pretending to flick long hair.'

'Oh, babe, your hair is lush!'

'They grabbed my bag and swung me round by it. I fell on the pavement, and then Adam Cummings kicked me in the stomach. They all thought it was hilarious. It wasn't until some old woman came storming up that they ran off.'

I could hear how shaken up Dom was.

'Oh my God! What is it about groups of lads when they get together?' I thought about the rednecks on the green bridge, yesterday, and the corridors at school. 'I hate Gareth and the rest of them! Dom, I'm so sorry. You don't deserve this. I wish I could give you a hug. At least with lockdown we don't have to go to school and face those idiots.'

'I'd be happy if I never had to go to school again.'

'Me too! Talking of which, have you done any schoolwork? I've hardly done any but have an idea for a history project.'

'I've done quite a lot. There's nothing else to do apart from watch films.'

'There's heaps to do here! Nan and I are making herbal medicine to help get Grandad better: I've been picking coltsfoot and butterbur. I've had this idea to photograph Grandad's woodwork and sell it online. It's amazing! He's so clever. You should see his workshop! It's stuffed full of all sorts of things he's made. There are wooden bowls, and boxes with lids, honey dippers and wooden spoons.'

'Yeah, I saw the photo you posted of you with your birthday present. Did he really make that?'

'He did. The photo doesn't really do it justice. You should see it! It's wonderful.'

'You should share more photos of what's going on there, Molly. It'd give us housebound townies something to look at.'

'What, and have everyone rip the piss out of me?'

'Stuff them! If you're going to start selling online, you need to build up the right following. People want to support small businesses. It's a big thing, you know. Just have a look on Etsy. It's where all the crafters hang out. My auntie sells sea glass jewellery there. I don't think Jess and her gang matter, do they?'

'Yeah, you've got a point.'

'There's this kid who had just got over 222K followers on Instagram because his dad said on Twitter he was getting bullied at school for making wooden bowls. He's got more orders than he can make now and was in the paper. I'll check out what hashtags he uses, and I'll ask Auntie Jean if she has any tips for getting set up on Etsy.'

'Brilliant! I'll start by tidying up his workshop and then take some product shots tomorrow.'

'Just listen to you, Molly! You sound so fired up.'

'Oh, I've got loads to do in the garden too. I'm helping Grandad plant the potatoes, and there are peas and beans to get in, and cabbages seeds to sow.'

'You know what you've got, don't you?'

'What? County bumpkinitis?'

'No, silly, you're creating a lifestyle brand. This is *hashtag*sustainableliving, and it's really in. Loads of people are starting to grow veg since lockdown started. We must think of a name for you.'

'Whoa! Steady, not so fast, Dom.'

'It's good to hear you so happy, Molly.'

'It's strange, Dom. If you forget the fact Grandad is so sick and we could all die of coronavirus, I suppose I am. Night, Dom.'

'Night, Molly.'

Seventeen

Busy Bee

Right. Schoolwork. It had to be done! I'd been getting nagging emails from all my teachers. Nan was out on her bike, doing her rounds, delivering stuff to people in the village, and I'd go and see Martha as soon as I could, but I had to get some work done to get school off my back.

The kitchen table was full of busy, with books, drawings, notebooks, gardening magazines and art stuff, so I made piles and put them on the settee next to Nan's sewing basket. A red thread caught my eye. It was carefully placed inside a leaflet tucked in the basket alongside the sewing Nan had shown me in the workshop when I first came to stay. I picked it up and read again of the Memorial Spoon Project, and of the woman Nan was honouring in her work, Ann Watson. Martha's mother. There was red thread around the amulet that belonged to Martha's mother, too.

I wondered what the connection with the red thread was, and how Nan had got Ann Watson's name? Did she ask for it, which if she did, did it mean Nan had some sort of control over all this, or did fate send it her way? Was there another power at work? What had Ann Watson done to be accused of witchcraft? The biggest question of all was, why was Martha here? What had caused her to stumble through the portal and for me to find her in the woods? It felt like the red thread was connecting us somehow. I had to know more, and I had to help her.

My history teacher, Miss Usher, was always encouraging us to do our own research, and had taken us to the archives at the Discovery Museum, so I sent her an email asking permission to do some digging into the story of Ann Watson and the other women. I'd already Googled her name, but nothing had come up apart from a list of those hanged for being a witch and the date, 21 August 1650. She got straight back to me:

Hello Molly,

I am delighted to hear from you. I do hope you and your family are keeping safe. The Newcastle Witch Trials of 1649 sound like a fabulous research project. It fits very nicely within the module that looks at the English Revolution, the Civil Wars and the death of Charles I. Can I suggest you look at the role of the Church and the State, and how it affected the working classes and the poor, especially women? Look at it from a social history point of view.

I have a friend who I worked with at the

university when I did my PhD, Jo Bath. You might like to look her up. She's written a book, *Dancing with the Devil and Other Tales of Northern Witchcraft*. You'll find it on Amazon. I'll drop Jo an email and put you two in touch. She may well have some information about your Ann Watson.

Molly, this is important work, and I salute you! Women's voices have been buried for centuries and it is our job to find out what happened, to let their stories be told. Do let me know where your research takes you and let me know if I can help any more.

Well done for using your initiative. Keep safe, Miss Usher.

I found a photo on the Northumberland archive's website of a list of names of folk put to death with the crimes they had committed. The writing was hard to make out, but there was Ann Watson, with the crime of being a 'wych' written in faded brown ink. With visits in person being out because of lockdown, I sent them an email, asking for any information they had about the witchcraft trials of 1649 and the subsequent hangings. I was interested in what happened in between the time Martha's mother was taken in 1649, and her hanging on 21 August 1650, eighteen months later. There were a few articles on the internet, and I went down a rabbit hole of research, learning about the seventeenth century, the plague, civil wars and how the belief of the Devil was as great as the belief in God, and how frightened everyone was of being punished for not being a devout Christian.

There was so much to find out, and it was all fascinating. There was a bit of information about the castle in Newcastle and the conditions in the dungeons. It was all so deeply shocking, and I was hungry to know more. I was only beginning to scrape the surface, but I was already reading of how women were abused. The more I read, the more I shook with anger. Then a horrid thought came crashing down. I sat back from the laptop and gasped, my hand over my mouth. I went cold as it dawned on me that Martha knew nothing of what was about to happen to her mother, and I was going to have to be the one who broke it to her. She had run away, as her mother insisted, following the banks of the Tyne until she stumbled through the portal and found us here. She had no idea her mother was going to be tortured in the dungeons for the next eighteen months, deprived of sleep, starved, marched up and down until she confessed to being a witch, then tried before a room full of men in nothing but her shift, stripped of all dignity, her private parts exposed for all to see, her body pricked with large pins to find the Devil's mark, then brutally murdered, hanged on the Town Moor. How on earth was I going to tell her that this was her mother's fate?

*

I still had maths, biology, French and geography to do, and was reluctantly opening up the work set in maths, when I was interrupted by Grandad messaging me on WhatsApp.

You busy Molly?

grandad! how are you feeling? can I call you?

No. Keep coughing. Sorry.

do you need anything bringing up?

No, keep away, Molly. Can you water the greenhouse?

done! watered it this morning

Thank you. So much I should be doing.

it's fine! let me know what else I can do

I can sow seeds or plant potatoes

Can't think straight. Head swimming. Ask Nan.

OK, grandad, rest up, love you 💚

This was just awful. Grandad should be outside, planting his own potatoes, not isolated upstairs, cut off from the world and too ill to go out in his precious garden. I knew how important growing his own veggies was and how much he'd be worried about not getting on. It sounded like he was getting worse, too. I'd always enjoyed gardening with Nan and Grandad when I was little, pulling carrots from buckets, and growing my own radishes and lettuces in a little square garden Grandad had made for me with rocks around the edge. How hard could this gardening lark be?

Grandad's gardening shed was stuck on the back of his

workshop. I didn't like going in there on my own, as I'd once seen a rat scuttling across a shelf. I opened the door carefully, banging it with my foot first. It was dark and gloomy in there and it had an earthy smell. I turned on the light. There were cobwebs over the windows, and it was a right tip with pots and soil, old seed packets, string, and tools all over the place. There was an old wooden school desk with a lift-up lid, where Grandad kept his seeds, so the mice didn't eat them, and a wooden thing and newspaper for making his own paper pots. I got a flashback. A memory I'd forgotten, of when I had been small, planting peas with Grandad. 'Night, night, peas!' we'd shouted together as we covered the seeds with soil in the little paper pots we'd made ourselves. I got a lump in my throat.

A well-thumbed book sat on a shelf, which I pulled down. *Gardener's Almanac.* There were worn pages and muddy thumb prints where it had been held. I placed my own thumb inside a muddy print of Grandad's, closed my eyes for a second and pressed it hard into the page.

The book gave gardening tips and advice on what to do and when, and how the phases of the moon were important. After the full moon, I read, up to the third quarter, it was time to plant crops that grew below ground. Potatoes! I would get the potatoes in for Grandad. On a shelf in a wire basket, high enough to keep the mice from them, were cardboard egg trays, and instead of eggs, they had potatoes with shoots coming from them.

I was just reaching up for one when a bird flapped in front of me and flew out the shed door. I nearly pooed my pants! I'd been watching out for rats and mice but hadn't figured on a bird being in the shed.

Its nest was up on one of the shelves inside a box that held gardening gloves and tools. I stood on my tiptoes and peered in. The nest was perfect, made from the smallest twigs and grass, with three speckled blue eggs nestled in the smooth inside. The bird must have just sat there, still as anything while I was rummaging around. I took a photo and sent it to Grandad. He messaged straight back with 'she makes her nest there every year'. I put up pictures of the sprouted potatoes (#gardening #potatoes #growersofinstagram) and the blackbird nest (#nature #bird #blackbird), and noticed that my full moon pictures had got loads of likes. I had a few new followers too, not the usual type, into makeup, influencers and shopping, but earthy sorts, and not all old like Nan and Grandad either. I followed them back, then I heard Nan putting her bike in the garage so went to tell her about the blackbird and my plan to plant the potatoes. She was cradling some weird-looking fungus in her arms that looked like a flying saucer.

*

'Birch polypore!' Nan announced, putting the fungus down on her workshop bench with great care. 'It grows on the trunks of birch trees, usually dead ones.'

It was large, round, with wavy edges, the colour of milky coffee on top and paler underneath. It was thick and creamy with spongey tubes that ran from top to bottom, and when she broke it in half it smelt strongly of mushrooms when they've been sitting in the fridge too long. Hadn't Martha talked about birch polypore too?

Nan reached for a book on her shelf, found the page

she was looking for. 'Aha! Just as I thought. Birch polypore is anti-viral as well as immune-boosting – time to make your Grandad some mushroom tea!'

I sniggered as I remembered a party last Christmas when someone made a pot of magic mushroom tea. We'd giggled for hours and talked a load of rubbish, but no one suffered any ill effects – well, apart from Dom, who had drunk two mugs and was tripping, so I had to sit with him for hours to make sure he was OK. I know my dad picked magic mushrooms too when he went off on his country walks in the autumn. We'd had 'the drug talk' at school and Mrs Thompson had asked if anyone's parents took drugs. I kept shtum. Didn't tell her my dad dried magic mushrooms in the airing cupboard!

We were looking up other remedies, and Nan was getting me to make a list so we could write up her Covid-busting potion in her version of the Gathering, when there was a knock at the door.

It was the vicar.

'Good afternoon, Sarah. And how do we find you?' He bent in a half bow, a simpering smile on his face. His voice was muffled due to the black face mask he was wearing. I could feel Nan bristling. If she were a dog, her hackles would have been up.

'We? Is there more than one of you?' Nan said, looking up the lane.

'Ha, ha! No, my dear, unless you mean the accompaniment of the Father, Son and Holy Ghost, who are always by our sides.' He grinned, cocking his head on one side.

'What do you want?' Nan barked. I stepped back, out

of sight but so I could still hear him. I hated it if someone called me 'dear'. It was so patronising.

'I've brought you a copy of the parish newsletter, Sarah. There is information about how the services will be going online. Have to march with the times, you know!'

'Great! We're running short of paper to light the fire.'

The vicar faltered, fumbled with the newsletter, which he held out to Nan, and seeing as she didn't take it, he bobbed down to leave it on the mat.

Nan could be so rude at times.

'Was there anything else?' Nan asked.

The vicar leant in, lowered his voice a little. 'Erm, I was wondering if you'd seen, erm, any, how shall I put it, undesirables around here of late?'

'How do you mean, "undesirables"?'

'Well, shall we say, homeless people.' He said 'homeless' like he had something in his mouth that tasted bad, and the 'o' like it was a capital O, all posh and condescending, like.

'And what would make you think being homeless made anyone undesirable?' Nan had her hands on her hips. If I were him, I'd have left while the going was good.

'Well, erm, some of the local landowners have been to see me. It would seem there has been some issues with trespassing. There have been reports of thefts: eggs from farms, clothing from washing lines, a saucepan, potatoes from Partridge Nest Farm's pantry, even jewellery. Someone was sure there was woodsmoke coming from the nature reserve, which is why we thought it might be a homeless person. You remember that refugee who camped in the woods last year in that little blue tent? All

165

that human excrement, utterly vile.'

'Utterly vile? Just listen to yourself!' Nan was shouting now. 'No, I haven't seen anyone, and if I did, they'd be welcome to a few eggs and potatoes and a good deal else besides.' Then Nan started quoting from the Bible! '"But if someone has material possessions and sees a brother or sister in need but refuses to help – how can the love of God dwell in a person like that?" Yes, I know my Bible, Vicar. Put that in your pipe and smoke it!'

'You are, of course, correct, Sarah, and the church does give to the poor, but we must keep harmony in our community, too. I can't have the local farmers up in arms over undesirables living on their land and stealing.'

'Oh, sod off! Don't darken my doorstep with your talk of undesirables. You're the only undesirable I can see round here.'

I peered around the door and could see the vicar had retreated into the lane.

'Oh, I see. I can understand your anger. You have always put others first, Sarah, and do so many good works within the village. Oh dear, I am in the most awkward position here. The farmers are most upset. Maybe I could say something in my next sermon about tolerance. Well, I won't keep you. Do come to the Easter Zooms. You'd be more than welcome.'

With that, Nan slammed the door in his face. 'Easter Zooms, my arse! Needs to grow a bloody backbone!' she said, then marched back into her workshop and started hacking at the mushroom.

Eighteen

Spite and Malice

With the mushroom tea brewing, Nan announced she was making Grandad's favourite blue cheese and wild garlic scones but needed me to go to the shop for her. They sounded well weird, but I played along with her as it gave me the perfect excuse to see Martha and warn her about the vicar's visit and the angry farmers. I'd get Grandad some Liquorice Allsorts, too. I used to always get him those on his birthday. Maybe Martha would like to come back and do some baking with us, and I could try and persuade her to come and stay again? She'd be so much safer at the cottage. I knew Nan would be OK about it.

While Nan was taking Grandad's brew upstairs, I raided the fridge for leftovers: I hacked off a chunk of cheese, grabbed a pint of milk and some bread, then tossed a couple of apples from the fruit bowl into my bag. I wasn't going to go empty-handed again. I started looking for something to pour the milk into and found a small plastic bottle in a big box of recycled containers. Mam and I just bought milk in plastic containers from the supermarket, but Nan had glass bottles delivered to the doorstep. Of course she did – no throwaway plastic here! She was right, of course. I'd watched *Blue Planet* too, with David Attenborough showing us how much plastic was in our oceans. Meg started her 'let's go for a walk' song, weaving in and out of my legs as I laced up my walking boots.

'Come on then, doesn't look like anyone else is going to walk you.'

I grabbed Meg's lead, put everything in a backpack and set off down the lane as fast as I could.

There was a queue at the shop, everyone spaced out two metres apart like the guidance said, and Martin the shopkeeper looked frazzled. He was stood on a chair waving his card terminal in the air when I arrived, swearing about the lack of signal. There were wooden picnic tables and chairs on the green in front of the shop, and it would seem they were doing a roaring trade in takeaway teas and coffees. Heads turned to look at me as I crossed the green and I saw a woman nudge her friend and say, 'She's her granddaughter, you know,' folding her arms and making a face like a chewed-up toffee. I glared at her and was about to say something when another woman with kind blue eyes came up and stood in between me and the gaggle of gossips. She was wearing a pretty face mask, with little pink flowers which matched her bright pink hair. She had a turquoise dress on and bright pink tights. What a contrast against the slurry of brown and beige that was sat around the wooden table.

'You're Molly, aren't you?' she asked, and crouched to stoke Meg.

I nodded yes and smiled. She looked friendly.

'Will you thank your gran so much for the tonic she sent? It seems to be doing the trick. Simon is so much better. She's so kind, your gran. You're very lucky to have her.'

'Who shall I say is thanking her?'

'I'm Julia,' she said. 'I live up the hill, over there.' She pointed to a row of houses, the windows reflecting as the sun hit them. Her blue eyes were soft and crinkled at the sides as she smiled. A friendly face at last in this sea of disapproval.

I tied Meg to a post, and when it was my turn, I asked Martin for blue cheese and the other things on my list, then asked if he had any toilet paper as I'd noticed we'd almost run out.

He put his fingers on his lips. 'Seeing as it's for Sarah and Joe, I'll make an exception. Don't tell that lot you've got some, though,' he said, nodding his head towards the women on the table who were clucking like Grandad's chickens. Martin shoved a two-roll pack of Andrex into a bag and tapped the side of his nose.

It was fairly obvious who they were talking about, as they kept looking at me.

'Erm, I'll have a takeaway hot chocolate too, please, Michael. I think I'll sit on the green a while, it's a long walk back.'

A woman, whose bony bum was perched on her seat like a crow on a branch, looked at me as I walked past. 'It's a disgrace!' she said, as I straddled the bench on a picnic table next to them. I pretended to be looking at my phone while I drank the takeaway hot chocolate but listened in to their gossip.

'They should do something about it, vagrants, thieves.'

'Used to be such a respectable village.'

'Do you think they're gypsies?'

'Utter pond life, filth.'

'I hear there's all sorts going missing. Mrs Greaves says her engagement ring is missing. Took it off to do the washing up and it's nowhere to be seen.'

'Nancy had washing disappear off her line, in broad daylight.'

'Our Conner is going out tonight with the lamps on the quad.'

'Aye, Nathan said he'd go too. They'll soon flush out whoever it is.'

'Won't be so keen to camp in our woods with a shotgun up their jacksies.'

I didn't wait to hear any more or to finish my hot chocolate. I hurried off towards the green bridge with Meg at my heels. I had to warn Martha.

*

I made sure no one saw us cross the bridge, then took the path that went along the top, through the darkness of the trees. I was glad I hadn't worn anything bright. I went as quietly as I could, and it was as if Meg sensed something was up too. She kept looking up at me, waiting for instructions, then crouching on the ground. When I was sure no one was watching, we ducked under the fallen tree covered in ivy and made our way to the beach. I paused by the water's edge and looked about and listened. The only sound was the water rushing by, gurgling over pebbles. I hopped over the stream. It was low, we hadn't had rain for ages and the rocks made excellent steppingstones.

Martha was nowhere to be seen. The fire wasn't lit, but her shelter was still there, and the few possessions she had. I didn't dare call out. I stood for a while, heart thumping and thoughts racing. Had she gone back through the portal? Had some of the locals already found her?

I slipped Meg's lead off. 'Go find Martha,' I whispered in her ear. Meg bounded off, jumping over bushes and brambles. I followed her as best as I could. There was no path. Meg gave one loud bark. I followed the sound, and there she was.

She was crouched behind some large stones, her hand over the dog's muzzle to stop her barking any more. Water rushed by over rocks in the river, a loud, urgent sound.

'I was so worried! Half the village is gunning for you.'

Despite the sun being high in the sky, Martha shook as she spoke and her teeth were chattering. 'I heard whistles, shouting, dogs barking, just like the other day but nearer. I did not wait to see if they made it over the water.' She panted as she spoke.

Martha's leggings were ripped and her legs bleeding. Her arms were covered in scratches, blood mixing with dirt. Her lips, dry and cracked, looked so sore.

'It's OK, there's no one in the woods, I've checked. Come on, back to the camp. I've brought food.'

Once back, I unpacked all the food I'd brought and laid it on the ground. Martha tore a chunk from the bread and bit into the cheese. Saliva dribbled down her chin, mingling with the dirt.

'What are you going to do?' I asked. 'You can't keep going on like this. Someone is going to find you sooner rather than later. Why don't you come back with me? I'm sure my nan would be cool. She's met you already and didn't bat an eyelid. She gave the vicar what for when he came round moaning about undesirables. They mean you, Martha. They want you gone.'

I told her about the gossiping women and the local thefts, the ring that had gone missing, and how all fingers were pointing at her, and how the local lads were going to flush her out.

Martha put her head on her knees, wrapped her arms around her head and started to cry. Through her sobs she said, 'Why me? Why is it happening again? I have done nothing wrong.'

'It's just not fair,' I said, and put my arm around her.

'They accused my mother of stealing. We were poor, but we never took what did not belong to us. Our neighbours gossiped about us too. Said we were the reason Goody Parson's milk had gone sour.'

'That's ridiculous! How can anyone make someone's milk go sour? Sounds like they forgot to put it in the fridge.'

'They said it was witchcraft. They say my mother has made a pact with the Devil. We are cunning folk, but we do not cast spells. Mother helps others, heals the sick, brings babies into the world with love, kindness and knowledge.'

'Do you really believe in the Devil?'

'Why, yes! Do you not?'

'I'm not sure I even believe in God.'

Martha clapped her hand over my mouth. 'You cannot say that! That's heresy. You would be hanged for sure.'

I peeled Martha's hand from my mouth. 'You really shouldn't do that, Covid rules and all that. But never mind, tell me more of what happened, Martha. What happened the day your mother was arrested?'

'Mother sells her potions and cures at the market, and I sell nosegays, sprigs of flowers and herbs. I only beg when we are desperate. I had not eaten that day and was hungry. I asked Goody Parsons for bread, and she started yelling in the market square about how my mother was a slattern and a Devil-worshipper, and how she brought our poverty on herself by not taking a man after Father died.' Martha's sobs had become desperate.

'Yes, but I don't understand. How does being poor and a single parent lead to her being accused of witchcraft?'

'Goody Parsons went home that evening to find her milk had turned sour. When the Bell Man came, asking for those who suspected their neighbours of witchcraft, Goody Parsons shouted my mother's name. She said she had cursed her household after she refused me food. Then others came forward, blaming my mother for putting curses on them, for stealing and being responsible for whatever ills the family were suffering.'

'Oh God, your poor mother. It's insane!'

'I know, they cannot accept us as we are. We are honest, God-fearing.'

'It sounds a bit like life round here. They don't like my nan much, just because she is different. She might be a bit peculiar, but she spends all her time trying to help others. Same goes for my so-called friends at school. I spend so much energy trying to fit in, and they just use me. I nearly got arrested too. You should hear what happened to my friend Dom, just because he's gay.'

But Martha was lost in her own thoughts, poking at the dead embers of the fire with a twig, her face streaked with tears. She couldn't go on like this. She was stick-thin, wrung out with emotion, barely surviving. Something had to be done. I was sick to death of other people judging, bitching and making life hell just because someone didn't fit the mould.

I needed to have a word with that vicar. He needed to calm everyone down instead of pandering to their prejudices. Undesirables? Enough was enough.

*

Instead of taking the usual path out of the woods I turned left once I'd ducked back under the fallen tree and came out of a gate onto the road that led up to the village. The field opposite was full of new-born lambs, but I was in no mood for perfect Instagram moments. I was fuming. I walked fast, angry words playing out in my head.

'Come on, Meg!' I called. 'Heel!' With my eyes fixed on the church at the top of the bank, I marched up the lane. It had started raining quite heavily, but that didn't bother me. It didn't sound like the vicar had done anything to calm the situation down. If anything, it felt like he'd already taken sides, and it wasn't on ours. He knew nothing of Martha. She needed our help. So much for the church doing good. Meg was lagging again, sniffing a patch of grass.

'*Heel!*' I yelled, then felt bad when she bounded up with worried eyes. I petted her neck. 'I'm sorry, I'm not cross with you,' I said, as I broke into a run.

As I ran, my leggings got wet where I splashed through puddles; I thought of all the people I knew who didn't fit the mould, how being 'different' was seen as something bad. I thought of Dom getting beaten up on Chillingham Road just for being himself, for being gay. I thought of all the times my so-called friends had ganged up on me, like when I was caught shoplifting and how everyone was laughing at me outside the Laing when the security guard caught up with me. I remembered the gossips and sniggers that had come behind hands in front of faces as I'd walked down the corridor at school after the party, and how I was called a slag. Then there was the photo I'd posted of me in the jumper Nan made and how they'd all been bitching about me on the group chat. I thought of Nan and Grandad and the stick they got in the village for having an alternative lifestyle and caring about the planet, and I thought of Martha and her mother: accused of being witches and having pacts with the Devil, just because they were poor and lived by themselves, and now Martha's mother was in jail and what was even worse, she was going to be hanged.

It had started to rain, and the sky wasn't the only place where dark clouds had gathered. By the time I got to the vicarage I was fizzing. There was a heavy brass knocker on the door, and I banged it for all I was worth. I waited a few seconds then banged it again.

The vicar came to the door, wiping his face on a serviette, his fat gut bursting in a black shirt that had food spilled down the front, the folds of his neck oozing from his white dog collar. There was food stuck in the corner of his mouth.

'I thought there was a fire, young lady! Why are you braying at the door like that?' He burped as he spoke, and there was alcohol on his breath.

'Call yourself a pillar of the community? You're a coward, that's what you are!'

The vicar stepped onto the path and looked up and down the village, then grabbed my arm and pulled me inside. 'Calm down, my dear. There's no need to shout. Won't you come in and share whatever is troubling you? Would you like a glass of water? It's Molly, isn't it?'

'No, I would not. And I'm not your dear. I've come to warn you to get those lads to back off. They've already given me grief today and I hear they're off to flush out your so-called "undesirable" from the woods. Why can't they just leave people alone?'

'I promised your nan I would try to smooth things over, Molly, you must trust me.'

'Well, I don't, and I don't believe you will, and anyway, even if you do mention something in your sermon or whatever, it'll be too little, too late. The whole village is gossiping and wagging its fingers. There's going to be trouble, and someone is going to get hurt!'

I didn't wait to hear any more. He knew I was right. I turned and marched back down the hill towards home. The rain came in sheets, driven by the wind, hitting us head on, which made walking hard. I had to grip on to my hood to keep it on. It was as if someone had ripped the sky open and was pouring tanks of water down. I couldn't have got any wetter. My hands were freezing, the rain like needles on my skin, and my socks so wet, my feet were squelching in my boots, water coming out through the lace holes. The lane was flooded in places, the water almost up to the top of my boots. Meg was shivering, her coat like a soggy sponge.

I was physically exhausted and emotionally wrung out. My head was done in. I'd tried to bring Martha back with me, but she wasn't having any of it. She was one stubborn girl. I was worried she'd disappear back through the portal, and that would be that.

Act Three

Flower Moon

Nineteen

Lost

The water poured off the porch roof in curtains as I lifted the latch and went in. As soon as I was through the door, Nan was there, hands on hips.

'Where have you been?' she shouted. 'I was worried sick! Haven't I got enough to worry about with your grandfather without you going missing as well?'

I was shivering with the cold, my dripping clothes making puddles on the flagstone floor. I was worried sick about Martha and needed her anger like a hole in the head.

'Nan, I need your help.'

'And I need yours! I've been up and down to Joe and have a mountain of orders to make up. Never mind keep gadding off for hours. Just look at the state of you!'

She sounded just like Mam.

'Never mind me, it's Martha. She's—'

The landline rang in the hall. Nan swore and said, 'What now?' and stomped out to answer it.

I peeled off my dripping socks, squeezing them out over the sink, then hung them over the bar of the Rayburn. I took off my leggings and put them to dry too, pulling a clean pair down from the rack that hung above the stove. My skin was white and mottled, and freezing cold to the touch. My stomach flipped as I thought of Martha. I found an old towel and gave Meg a good rub-down. She rolled on her back on the warm mat, belly to the air. It was speckled with dirt.

'You scruffy old thing,' I said, rubbing her tummy. 'It's alright for you! Not a care in the world.'

I could hear Nan's voice raised in the hallway and went to the closed door to listen.

She was shouting, 'He is not going, and that's that!'

I guessed it was Mam. Nan must have cut her off as the door handle turned and she burst through, almost knocking me flat.

'That was your mother. She wants to call an ambulance for Joe.'

'Is he that bad?'

'He's not good, Molly. He is struggling to get his breath and I can't seem to get his temperature down.'

'Then call one!'

'If he goes in, I'm afraid he won't come out.'

'Yes, but if he stays here, then that might be the end of him altogether.'

'Oh, just say it how it is, won't you, Molly? You sound just like your mother.'

'This is serious, Nan, Grandad could die!'

I was shouting at her, and she was shouting at me. This was just horrid.

Nan turned around, muttering something about peas in the pod, opened her workshop and disappeared down the steps, slamming the door behind her. I heard the key turn in the lock. Fine! I didn't want to talk to her either. She was being ridiculous.

I went upstairs out of earshot and rang Mam straight back.

'Nan is impossible! She's locked herself in the workshop,' I said as soon as she picked up.

'Tell me about it! I've had a lifetime of her. I'm going to try and get you an oxygen tank delivered. If he gets any worse you dial 999, do you hear me? Molly?'

'Yes, Mam.'

'Molly, are you OK?'

'No, not really.'

'Is it just Nan and Grandad, or is there anything else? Apart from the obvious, missing your friends and life here. I saw Jess's mam at Aldi the other day. She says Jess is missing you. Jess said you hadn't been answering her messages.'

'Jess can take a hike! I'm so over her.'

'Oh, Molly, you've been friends since primary school. Don't let this pandemic get in the way. Times are very strange. We need our friends. Look, I've got to go. Ring me back anytime, day or night, if Dad gets any worse. These next twenty-four hours are critical. We'll just override your nan and get that ambulance rang.'

'Mam, before you go, there is something else. I've met this girl, it's a long story, but she's in trouble. She's on the run, and now she's gone missing.'

'Have you rung the police?'

'No, it's complicated. I can't ring the police.'

'If she's a missing person, you can, Molly. It's not your responsibility.'

But it was. I did feel responsible. It was me who found her when she'd come through the portal, and it was me who had to help her. The police were the last people I wanted involved.

'OK, Mam, I hear you. Don't worry. I'll do the right thing.'

'I'm sure you will, Molly. Now, I must go, but if your grandad deteriorates any more, you ring me back, do you hear?'

'Yes, Mam. I will.'

'I'm super proud of you, Molly. You know that?'

'Bye, Mam, love you.'

My voice croaked as I got those last words out. She was proud of me. When did I last hear that? I missed her so much. I'd been so angry with her when she sent me here, but now I was beginning to understand. It wasn't just the lockdown stuff and why I had to come here, but I was beginning to see just how much she'd had to put up with, always working so hard, trying to bring me up with a feckless dad who just wanted to have fun and get trollied all the time. It wasn't like her parents were much support either. Nan seemed to be stuck in a rebellion groove, and Grandad, well, as lovely as he was, never said boo to a goose.

*

I sat down on the bed. The rain was still battering the windows, and I was shaking. I felt light-headed, as if I were floating. The room had gone all swimmy, and then I realised I hadn't eaten since breakfast so went downstairs. The radio was on in the kitchen, and I listened as the news came on. It gave the number of deaths from coronavirus, and the number of people in hospital. It was in the thousands. I stood still, holding on to the edge of the table as I listened. It was all so frightening. Maybe Grandad would be joining those statistics soon? Boris Johnson was making another announcement. Lockdown would be extended for another three weeks. That was fine with me, I was in no rush to go back to town. I was needed here. My stomach growled. I was definitely hungry.

'Would you like me to cook tea?' I called through the workshop door. It came out quite passive aggressive. There was no reply, so I opened the fridge. The Müller Lights Mam had bought at Morrison's were in the back of the fridge, way past their sell-by date. It occurred to me that I hadn't thought about dieting or weighed myself since I'd come, and hoyed them in the bin. Then I fished them out again, laughing at myself. I emptied the synthetic gloop down the sink and rinsed them out. They'd make good plant pots if I bashed holes in the bottom for drainage.

I didn't feel any fatter, even though I'd eaten more cake in the last couple of weeks than I had the whole of last year. I'd stopped sneaking food too. I didn't need to hoard sweets and crisps. There was no shame in this house over food. It was to be enjoyed.

There was hardly anything to eat in the fridge, so I put on a coat and some wellies and sloshed down the soggy garden. I noticed the downpipe on the shed had come loose and water was flooding the path down to the veg patch. Another job to add to the ever-growing list! There were lots of leeks, some sprouting broccoli, and brightly coloured chard, with ruby-red and yellow stems. I'd make a stir fry. I traipsed back in across the sodden grass, with an armful of muddy vegetables. What had happened to me? I wouldn't have touched muddy vegetables with a barge pole a few weeks ago. Before I went into the back door, the roar of the water in the burn caught my attention. Instead of the trickle of clear water it had been during these dry weeks, it was a surging torrent of brown water. You could hear the knocking sound of boulders being washed downstream with the force of the water. If it got much higher, we'd need to put sandbags by the front door. I remember Grandad telling me about Storm Desmond, and how the river had risen to being within a couple of centimetres of flooding the house. The front door was lower than the road, so if the burn burst its banks, then it would pour in.

I was just about to go into the garage to check if there were any sacks to make into sandbags when I heard a quad on the lane. I was used to hearing the farmer's quad bike, but it was the sound of shouting and cheering that drew my attention. There were three lads: two were balanced on the backplate, and Matt, David's son, was driving. Two large black dogs ran alongside, barking. They roared past the house and up the hill to the farm, punching the air and laughing. One of them fired a shotgun into the sky. They seemed to have something to celebrate.

Martha! I had no choice. I had to go back out.

*

Up in my bedroom I changed into the warmest clothes I could find and stuffed some spare ones for Martha into a carrier bag to keep them dry, and then into a backpack. It was getting dark, and the rain was hitting the window hard. It was as if someone was throwing buckets of water at the house. I had to hurry. Had the lads found Martha? Was she hurt? I couldn't bear to think of her out there, cold, wet, frightened, all alone and in real danger. I had to find her and bring her home, and I would have to do it on my own. Nan was no help, and there was no way I was ringing the police. Not yet anyway.

I found a head torch and a pair of waterproof trousers in the cupboard under the stairs and a big waterproof coat of Grandad's that came down to my knees. It smelt of him, earthy and musty. There were bits of string and a packet of lettuce seeds in the pocket with a mint humbug that had gone sticky and was covered in grit. In an inside pocket was a small plastic pouch, and in it, the remains of a packet of Golden Virginia tobacco, some rizlas and a lighter. I felt a stab of pain in my chest as I held them and felt my loyalties torn between Grandad and Martha. Who needed me the most? What if Grandad took a turn for the worst while I was out? But I was the one who had to help Martha. I would go, find Martha, drag her back if I had to, then come back and check on Grandad. Meg was out for the count on the mat by the Rayburn, so I left her sleeping and slipped out of the front door without a sound.

The wind was behind me this time, but just as strong. It had an urgency about it, as if it were pushing me on, telling me to go, to hurry. I didn't feel as cold as before, as I was well wrapped up and in waterproofs from head to toe. It would be social suicide if I walked around town looking like this, but out here there was no one to judge, and I congratulated myself on how practical I was these days. The head torch was great and lit up the lane, which looked very different at night. Trees bent and broke, leaving debris in the road, branches threatening to crack and break over me. The water was flowing down the lane in rivers, splashing back in waves, and in places it was completely flooded. I made it to the nature reserve and hurried down the path towards the fallen tree. It didn't occur to me to be frightened by the shapes and shadows, and I was getting to know the path so well that I stepped over the tree roots and ducked under fallen trees without having to shine the torch on the ground.

I stopped in my tracks when I got to the water's edge. Just like the burn in the garden, the stream had risen to a surging torrent, metres wide, and there was no sign of the steppingstones. I stood on the bankside with the wind and rain whipping my hair and yelled Martha's name at the top of my voice. But there was no way she'd hear me over the raging river. I knew she was still around. I don't know how, but I felt it inside, and it was up to me to find her.

Whilst this was only a side shoot of the main river, it would still have been madness to cross, so I decided to search the rest of the nature reserve. I went down as far as you could before you got to the barbed-wire fence and the keep out sign the farmer had put across the way. I then doubled back and went as far as I could in the other direction, through the pine trees, calling Martha's name all the time. The sounds were different here, where the trees were dense, like a train in a tunnel. It was drier too, and a welcome relief from the driving rain. There was no sign of her, so I hurried back towards the stream, trampling over wild garlic, not keeping to the footpath. The smell of garlic filled the air and what with the knots in my stomach, worrying about Martha and all the running, I felt sick. I doubled over on the bank and heaved. My legs shook. There was nothing for it: I would have to go across the water and search the island.

Twenty

The Rescue

The roar of the water in the main part of the river, just the other side of the island, was deafening, threatening, like a beast that had been unleashed. It sounded closer than it was in the dark. The stream here had risen and was much wider than before, but I reckoned I could cross it. The rain continued to drum down on the leafy canopy, and all around there was an earthy smell, as the water tore up the mud from the bank and carried it away, surging, downstream. I was shaking inside, but I knew I had to be strong. I shone my head torch beam onto the opposite bank. In the darkness, the water looked black, menacing. I grabbed on to an overhanging branch and took a deep breath. The first few steps were OK, the water only knee-deep, but I was surprised at just how cold the water was as it soaked through my clothes and wrapped around my legs. I looked again at the bank opposite, lit by the light of my torch. That was my aim. I had to keep that in my sights. I nosed my toes gently over weeds and plants, trying not to get them tangled. I felt them slip and slide on greasy stones. My lower legs were now numb, the cold of the water no longer a problem, but then the ground underneath my feet gave way and I slipped, landing hard on a stone on my backside, the water up to my armpits. I fell back, taking in a mouthful of muddy river water, and gasped as the shock of the cold water took my breath away, the force of the current threatening to take me away too. I could feel my legs being pulled downstream, but I braced myself, digging my feet hard onto the riverbed, shifting my centre of gravity forwards and down. I mustered every ounce of strength I had and stood up again. I could feel the rocks under my feet, some slippery with slime, some moving with the force of the water, bashing into my legs, threatening to knock me off my feet. Now the water was waist-deep. *Breathe, Molly, breathe.* I regulated my breathing, and the panic went away. If I kept my feet wide, planted to the bottom, it was OK. I could see there was another overhanging tree on the other side, just a metre away; I'd make a grab for that. I had to hang on. I had to stay upright, keep my balance, or the water would sweep me away. Careful to take small steps and not lose my footing, I made it to the other side and tried to haul myself up onto the bank.

I was exhausted, and the water wanted to hold me in its grasp. I planted two hands onto the bank but only got fistfuls of soft mud, my hands slipping back down the bank. I grabbed at tufts of grass only to have them come away in my hands. I scrabbled around for tree roots, anything to grab on to so I could haul myself up, but I kept slipping back, being washed a bit further downstream with the force of the water. At last, I grabbed on to something which didn't come away but screamed as thorns dug into my hand. I was past caring and my hands so numb with cold I held on. It was a bramble, perhaps, but it didn't come away and I was able to get a good footing on a lower bit of bank and crawled out on my hands and knees. I was clear of the water. I'd made it! I lay panting for a while but knew I must keep moving. I stood up, my legs shaking with exhaustion, and cried out as my ankle turned on a fallen wet branch I hadn't seen in the dark, and my leg folded underneath me. I landed awkwardly, jarring my knees and bashing my leg on something hard, a rock, maybe. I hollered with pain, holding my foot. It was agony, and I was freezing. I burst into tears, my shoulders shaking with sobs, and sat there in a heap. I yelled for Martha to come and help me, but there was only the sound of the rain and the river. What was I going to do? Where was Martha? I screamed her name again, snot mingling with tears. She had to come and help me! I tried to stand. It was so painful, and I yelped every time I put my foot on the ground, but somehow, I managed to hobble the short distance to the camp.

I was too late. The lads had got there first. Charred pieces of wood from Martha's fire had been kicked all around by big boots that had left footprints in the mud. Martha's shelter was torn down, and her few possessions had been hurled about, stamped on. I picked up the pieces of her wooden bowl, broken in two. I called again. But there was no sign of Martha. She was long gone. She wasn't even on the island. I was kicking myself for crossing that water.

My teeth were chattering, and I was shivering. My clothes were wet. I was so cold. I needed to get back but couldn't put any weight down on my right foot. I grabbed a branch and used it as walking stick and limped down to the water's edge, but there was no way I was going to get across in this state. I didn't have the strength to fight the water. It had been madness to cross the first time; it would be suicide to do it again. There was nothing for it – I'd have to phone for help.

I reached for my phone which was in the pocket of my waterproof coat. But the coat was so waterproof, the pocket was like a goldfish bowl, my phone bobbing about in river water. I had drowned my phone. I was stuck on the island, injured, with no way of contacting anyone. I called, 'Help!' a few times, but the rushing water was making such a din that even if someone was out in the woods, which I very much doubted, they'd never have heard me.

Think, Molly, think…

I had to get warm. I was soaked to the skin. *The spare clothes!* I ripped open the top of the rucksack, half expecting the spare clothes I'd brought for Martha to have been ruined when I fell in the water, but they were amazingly dry. Thank goodness I'd double-wrapped them in plastic. I leant onto a tree for support. My ankle was killing me, and I was shaking all over, my teeth chattering. I started to whimper as I peeled off my wet clothes, my skin cold, as bare flesh was exposed. The dry clothes helped a bit, but I was still frozen.

Grandad's lighter! I felt inside the coat. It was still there, the baccy and papers dry thanks to the waterproof lining and plastic pouch. I clicked the lighter a few times. It worked! If only I'd put my phone in there! I crawled on all fours, with my bad foot in the air, and moved the fallen branches that had been the roof of Martha's camp and found some dry sticks. I remembered she'd kept a small wood pile at the back to keep it dry. It had stopped raining, and with the torn-up rizla packet, the dry sticks and a working lighter, I managed to get a fire going. Still crawling, saving my hurt ankle, I went backwards and forwards into the den and made a pile of semi-dry wood and hauled out the rushes Martha had used as a bed. The wood was damp and there was a lot of smoke, but it was going, and I would be able to get warm.

The dry wood and rushes weren't all I found at the back of the den. Under Martha's makeshift bed was the Gathering! It was still in its cloth bag. I held it to my chest as if it were a long-lost friend and stared into the flames. It answered one question: Martha couldn't have gone back through the portal. She'd have taken the Gathering with her.

*

I sat on the ground by the fire and added branches and sticks until it blazed hot, crackling, sending sparks into the air. Despite a cold wind on my back, the front of my body was warming up, my cheeks glowing. I thought of Martha, how she would have sat here, night after night, adding sticks to the fire, worrying in case someone saw the smoke, keeping it as small as she could. My fire could be huge – it didn't matter. The bigger the better: someone might see it, though who, I had no idea. It must have been close to midnight by now. I thought how frightened Martha must be, lost in time, no doubt worried sick about her mother locked in the city gaol, not knowing of her fate. I wondered if she'd stay here in our time or go back through the portal? I knew her mother was murdered on 21 August 1650, hanged by the neck on the Town Moor, alongside fifteen other women and one man, accused of witchcraft. I decided there and then that I owed it to Martha to tell her when I found her. She had a right to know what was about to happen to her mother. I wondered what the stories of the others hanged that day were. Were they, like Martha and her mother, outsiders, victims of gossip, a bit like Nan and me? Not fitting in, trying to live lives that were different from others, which made them stand out from the crowd? I suddenly felt very proud of my nan and grandad, doing their bit for the planet. They were trying hard to live sustainable lives, growing their veg, healing folk with herbs and kindness, sharing what they had. I wanted to be like them. They were good people. There was no doubt in my mind that Martha and her mother were good people too.

While I had been sitting there thinking, it had stopped raining and the clouds were clearing. A half-moon shone through the gaps in the clouds, and silver light showed on patches of ground. I turned my head torch off and looked up to the moon. It felt like a friend. I thought of Jess and my friends in town. The same moon would be shining on them. What would they say if they could see me now? For once, I didn't care.

I must have fallen asleep at some point as I woke to the sound of barking. I shivered in the damp early morning air and tried to stand, but my ankle was swollen and painful. I winced and pulled up my trouserleg. My ankle was black and blue.

Just then I heard a shrill dog whistle and a voice calling a dog to heel. A figure loomed through the mist: tall and male. I could hear other dogs barking and another man's voice, calling my name.

'It's OK, I've found her!'

'Get away from me!' I shouted, and as I reached for a stick, I saw Matt coming through the mist. I inched back, afraid of what was coming next. Was he bringing his group of rednecks for some fun at my expense?

What came next was totally unexpected. Meg flew past Matt and jumped onto my lap, turning circles, licking my face, singing a dog song.

'Good dog!' another man's voice said. I recognised his voice, but it wasn't until he stood in the clearing that I could see it was David Thompson, Nan's farmer neighbour from up at the castle.

'Well, don't just stand there, give her your coat, you useless fool!' David shoved his son on the shoulders, and he took off his coat, all the time avoiding any eye contact with me.

A few seconds later, a stiff waxed cotton coat was being wrapped around me that smelt of aftershave, mingled with animals and farms.

'You're safe now, Molly, let's get you home.' David scooped me up into his arms and carried me out of the camp.

'The Gathering!' I said. 'Er, I mean, my book! Can you pass it, please?'

'This?' Matt said, holding the Gathering out to me.

'Yes.' I snatched it from him. 'Can you pass that bag too, please?'

I wrapped the Gathering in the plastic bag and put it safe in my rucksack. I wasn't going to let it out of my sight.

'How did you know I was here?' I asked as I was carried down to the water's edge.

'This lad and his idiot friends had clearly been up to no good when they got in. It was my wife who dragged the story out of them. Seems they'd decided to do some vigilante work, flushing out whoever it was camping over here in the island. Then your nan rang. Worried sick about you. Said you were missing, said you'd been telling her someone called Martha was in trouble, and we put two and two together. It was your dog, Meg who led us to you. She knew where you were.'

'What about Martha?' I said, glancing back at the camp over David's shoulder as he carried me down to the river.

'You mean it were a lass camping out here? We thought it was some homeless bloke,' Matt said.

His father glared at him. 'Well, it wasn't. It was Martha, and she's only my age. She's my friend, and I'm even more worried about her now.' I glared at Matt too. 'You didn't seem over friendly towards me when you saw me on the bridge the other day, so why would it bother you that she is a girl? Or were you just showing off in front of your mates?'

'Matt?' his father asked, looking for an explanation.

'God, we never realised. Er, I mean, I'm sorry, Molly. I've been a right jerk, haven't I? Don't worry, the lass won't have gone far in this weather. We'll have a good search for her, the lads and me. We'll soon find her.'

*

Nan was waiting under the porch when we pulled up on the quad bike, me balanced with one butt cheek on the backplate, holding on to David for support. Nan's arms were folded across her chest. I was trying to read her expression. Her hair was all over the place, and there were bags under her eyes. It looked like she'd been up all night.

'Oh, my precious,' she said, touching my arm then standing aside as David carried me into the house, ducking in the low doorways. He lowered me gently down on the settee. Nan came and sat next to me, careful not to touch my leg. Matt stayed outside.

'Thank goodness you're safe,' she said, and I melted into her arms. She stroked the back of my head and I allowed myself to let go. My shoulders heaved and the tears flowed. She cried too. 'I'm so sorry,' she said.

'What have you got to be sorry about? I was the one who nicked off in the middle of the night.'

'But to search for your friend. Molly, I'm so proud of you. I am so sorry I didn't listen.'

'I'd better be off, Sarah,' David said.

'Thank you for bringing her home, David. Now, where's that son of yours? I want to give him a piece of my mind.'

'Not now, Nan,' I said. 'Let them go.'

David and Matt set off on the quads in search of

Martha. There was nothing I could do to help. I melted into the soft cushions of the settee.

The warm kitchen had never felt more like home. After giving me a steaming mug of hot chocolate and a fried egg sandwich, Nan sat down and took my ankle in her lap. It was very bruised, as were my legs where the rocks had bashed into them. She rubbed a balm into them from a jam jar.

'What's in this, Nan?'

'Comfrey, the great healer, arnica for the bruising, rosemary to bring warmth back and lavender for pain.'

Nan put a knitted blanket over my knees, tucking me in as if I were a child. Tears rolled down my cheeks.

'How's Grandad?' I said. 'And what about Martha?' I cried big sobs. It was all such a mess.

'Shush, Molly, rest your eyes. Everything will be just fine. David and the lads will go and look for Martha, and your grandad, well, he's much the same, but I'm keeping an eye on him. He has been taking my medicine and back-to-back paracetamol and ibuprofen. Last time I checked he was sleeping. I'll tell him you're back when he wakes. Now rest.'

Twenty-One

Martha's Story

The grandfather clock woke me with three loud chimes. I'd been asleep for hours! I felt for my phone but then remembered. I'd drowned it. I wanted to message Mam and ring Grandad to see how he was. I called out to Nan, to see if she was in her workshop, but the only sound was the ticking of the clock. I lay back on the settee, confused, my head swimming. I still blamed myself for not going back for Martha after I'd talked to the vicar. If only I'd got her to see sense and come back here. I wondered if David and Matt had found her yet. Or if she had gone back, back in time. I looked down at the floor for my bag, but Nan had emptied it, and it hung from the rack about the Rayburn. She will have found the Gathering, then.

I got up slowly and limped to the bottom of the stairs: I had a terrible headache and my legs felt weak and wobbly. I held on to the banister and called up, but there was no reply. Grandad must be asleep. My ankle wasn't too bad as long as I didn't put all my weight down in it, but I spotted an old walking stick in the umbrella stand by the front door, so I took that and hobbled across the kitchen to the back door.

The sun was high in a deep blue sky, the trees full of pink apple blossom, the garden full of birdsong. I could see Nan down the garden path, stood in the middle of her herb garden. But she was not alone. There, right next to her, was Martha. They were talking about plants, pointing to different herbs.

'Martha!' I called.

'Molly!'

Martha ran down the garden and we hugged each other tight.

'Look who I found in your grandad's woodshed!' Nan said, coming down the path with a basket of herbs and flowers.

'What happened?' I asked. 'Are you alright? I came looking for you. I got stuck on the island!'

I had so many questions. We went into the kitchen and sat around the table while Nan busied herself in the workshop. I made a pile of toast and two hot chocolates and listened while Martha told me what had happened.

'I was sheltering from the rain when I heard a great roaring. I thought it was a monster.'

'Do you mean the sound of the river? It was so high!'

'No, that was terrifying too, but this was different. It was not a sound I had heard before. I could see through the trees, three men on a machine that moved. It made such a noise. I have never seen such a beast. I was petrified.'

'That'll have been the quad bike,' I said, reaching for a slice of toast and jam.

'Then I heard loud bangs, like a musket being fired, only louder.'

'Yeah, they had shotguns with them. You must have been terrified. Here, have some more toast.' I pushed the plate towards her.

'Thank you. This is very good.' Martha spread her slice with strawberry jam and licked her fingers. 'I walked to the very end of the island then waded over the water and hid amongst the bushes. It was deep, but I got across. The men didn't see me. They had gone over to my camp. I could hear them, shouting, breaking my shelter. I was so frightened. I should have come with you when you offered.'

'I went up to that vicar's after I left you. Gave him a piece of my mind. I should have come and tried to get again you after that. I'm sorry I left you there, Martha. I didn't see you on the lane, though?'

'I did not walk along the lane for fear of being seen. I went through the fields, followed the path of the silver hare.'

'The silver hare?'

'Yes, I believe the same hare that guided me through the portal showed me the way here. It ran in front of me, through fields of grass, through gaps in hedges. It was dark, but somehow the hare glowed with a silver light. I had to crawl through a hawthorn hedge, look!' Martha showed me the scratches up her arms and on her face. 'It was dark and raining, but the hare kept me in its sight, and I just followed.'

'Show me your arm again,' I said.

Martha held her arm out, and I pulled off some strands of silver thread, caught in the sleeve. We looked at the thread and each other. I had seen silver fluff, silver thread, beads, bits of shiny stuff before, each time in places the hare had been. I had picked up some of them. They were in a dish by my bed.

'So, how come Nan found you in Grandad's shed?'

'I remember you showed me your grandfather's workshop when I visited on your birthday. I was too afraid to knock on the door of the house, and it seemed a good place to hide. I made a fire in the stove. I was so cold. I was able to get dry and warm. I even found a packet of—'

'Digestives!' I said. 'Grandad always has a couple of biscuits with his cup of tea. I'm so pleased you came here, Martha.'

'I knew I would be safe here.'

'Gave me such a fright,' Nan said, coming out of her workshop. 'Thought it was Joe for a minute, when I saw the smoke coming out of his workshop chimney!'

*

I made us all another cup of tea, and Nan joined us around the table. She carried two volumes with her from the workshop: the Gathering and her own leather-bound book. That's not all she brought out. On top of the two books, like a crown on a cushion, was the piece of fabric she was stitching for the Memorial Spoon Project, the piece of embroidery with Martha's mother's name: Ann Watson. It was time to talk to Martha about her mother.

There was an awkward silence at first. Martha's eyes widened when she saw the fabric, with her mother's name. Nan picked it up and handed to her. Martha looked back at Nan, her chin trembling, tears brimming in her eyes.

Running her fingers over the red letters, embroidered in chain stitch, she said, 'This date, 1650, is that my mother's death?'

Nan reached for Martha's hand and squeezed it tight. I held on to her other hand. Nan looked at me, raised her eyebrows and nodded gently. Had Nan known all along that Martha wasn't from our time?

'Yes, Martha,' I said. 'I've found your mother's name in a list at the archives.'

Martha gasped. I continued. It was hard. 'There's no easy way of saying this, Martha. I'm so sorry. It would appear she was hanged on 21 August 1650 along with fifteen others. There were fifteen women in total, including your mother and one man, all accused of witchcraft.'

Martha sucked in the air in tiny gasps. She looked like a baby bird that had fallen out of the nest. 'What else do we know?' she asked.

'We know that she was innocent of witchcraft, that she was a victim of malicious gossip and fear of God and the Devil. We know the witchfinder was a fraud and was himself tried later.'

'That's of no help to your mother, though, of course,' Nan said.

We sat in silence; the only sound in the room was the ticking grandfather clock. Tears fell down Martha's cheek, as she sat with her head bowed. It was as if she had known all along this would be her mother's fate.

After a while, Nan broke the silence. 'I believe we are connected, Martha, somehow, somewhere down the line. I don't have my family tree and have no evidence to say we are related, but the similarities in your Gathering and my grandmother's book are many. I believe our coming together is not a coincidence.'

Nan placed the two volumes side by side. Both bound in brown leather, both with a crescent moon on the front. Both with drawings, notes, recipes: loose pieces of paper, bits of fabric and pressed flowers. One written in Old English, the writing impossible to make out, the other easier to read, but much of the writing old-fashioned, with loops and swirls. Both books so very precious.

'I felt it as soon as I held it,' I said. 'It was like an electric current running up my arms, and I can feel it now, as we hold each other's hands.'

I reached for Nan's free hand around the table, forming a circle, and I was right. You could feel the power, feel the energy, flowing between us three.

Then the phone rang, bringing us crashing back down the earth. It was Mam. She'd been trying to get me on my mobile, but of course, that was now sitting in a bag of rice drying out in the warming oven of the Rayburn.

While I talked to her on Nan's landline, Nan went upstairs to help Grandad, who was having a coughing fit.

'I can't talk for long, Mam, Martha's here.'

'Martha? Molly, it's against the law to mix with other households. We are in lockdown!'

'Don't shout, Mam. I know it's lockdown, but Martha's come from the seventeenth century. She hasn't been near the rona!'

'Have you gone insane like my mother?'

'No, and I know it sounds mad, but it isn't. It's all perfectly sensible. You see, there is this portal, and a hare, and silver thread, and the Gathering and—'

'Molly! Enough! I cannot take this all in right now. I have a ward that is bursting at the seams, and staff off sick. I've phoned because I was worried. I couldn't get in touch with you or Mam. I need to know how my Grandad is.'

'Nan's up there now. He was having a coughing fit. She's taken up a bowl of vapours for him. We're going to try some lobelia, wild cherry bark and hawthorn berries in the next batch of medicine. Martha knows tons about herbalism too – her mother healed the sick, even stopped her and Martha getting the Plague, but she's going to be hanged for being a witch.'

'Oh, good grief! Molly. That's quite enough. Your grandad needs proper treatment. Enough of witches and herbs. I know it's been difficult for you, but no more talk of your imaginary friend.'

'But Mam—'

'No, Molly! Grandad is going to die unless my mother stops this nonsense and sees sense. As for you—'

I gently replaced the phone onto its base, cutting her off. I'd heard enough.

Twenty-Two

Beltane

There was a moment in between sleep and being fully awake, when the warmth of my bed, the softness of my duvet and the quietness all around kept me suspended in pink fluffy clouds. Then I heard the bark of Grandad's cough coming through the floorboards from the attic above and sat bolt upright. As I listened to him, the pink fluffy clouds skidded away, and grey skies gathered. Maybe Mam was right. Maybe we should phone for an ambulance. It was awful. I winced with every cough and could feel my anxiety levels going through the roof, my heart beating in my chest, my fingers all trembly. It wasn't just Nan who wanted to keep him here; he was being just as stubborn. Maybe I had to overrule them, take charge?

Martha had insisted she sleep in Grandad's workshop. She said she didn't want to be a burden, not that she was, and that she was plenty warm enough out there. We were all so tired last night, I reckon we could have slept on a spike, so we just let her go and make herself comfy.

I could hear Nan downstairs: there was music on and she must have been sweeping the floor. I could hear her knocking the broom against the cupboards. I wouldn't miss her clattering around at the crack of dawn when I went back to town! Why she could never keep quiet in the mornings, I do not know, and what on earth did she have to sing about? Grandad could be dying! I had no way of knowing what the time was, with my phone out of action.

'Morning, poppet! Beltane greetings!' Nan said, as I hobbled into the kitchen grabbing my arm in the crook of her arm and swinging me around to some dum-diddly music she was playing.

'Ouch! Mind my foot!' I side-stepped over to the kitchen worktop away from her prancing.

'Oh, I love the Peatbog Faeries, don't you? Just listen to those bagpipes!'

'Never heard of them, and Nan, why are you leaping around to music when Grandad is at death's door? And why have you got flowers in your hair?'

'It's May Day, darling, Beltane, the time when the earth is waking up and new life is springing forth. The veil is thin! We can connect with the spirits!'

I stood there, shaking my head in disbelief. She was barking mad.

'This is all for Joe, you nelly. Come on, we've got lots to do.' Nan started whizzing around the kitchen again, and I stopped her. Put my hand on her arm.

'I think we should call an ambulance. I could hear him though the floor. He sounds dreadful.'

'No, Molly! Give it another day. He's no worse than he was yesterday. Maybe his body is battling the virus? If he's no better by tomorrow, then yes, we can call an ambulance, but there's lots we can still do for him today. Now, I want you to—'

'Oh, Nan,' I huffed, wincing with the pain in my ankle as I opened cupboards, getting a cup and bowl out, 'can I at least have some breakfast and get dressed?'

'Yes, Miss Grumpy Pants, you can, but I do need your help for this to work.'

Nan wanted me to collect lots of hawthorn blossom from the hedges down the lane. She seemed to have forgotten I was in pain, but I managed. I didn't have to go far. I took the wheelbarrow, as it was hard to carry with its sharp prickles. I filled jugs of water and packed them with the sweet-smelling blossom, bringing them into to kitchen. It looked so pretty with its tiny little white flowers.

'No! Not indoors,' Nan shrieked, pushing me back out.

'What?' I asked.

'Not indoors!' Nan said. 'It's bad luck to bring hawthorn inside. Now, I want you to make a path with flowers either side down to the firepit. Can you get Martha to help you? Have you seen her this morning? We'll have a proper Beltane fire ceremony tonight. We must have hope, Molly!'

*

I took some toast and jam out to Martha, who was already up, looking at all the wooden pieces Grandad had made.

'These are beautiful,' she said, holding a wooden mushroom.

'They are, and I keep meaning to take some photos and sell them online for him, but I just haven't got round to it.'

'They would sell in the marketplace, I am sure,' Martha said.

'Yeah, he did sell them in Hexham, before the pandemic. All that stopped in lockdown, but it's starting up again. That's another reason to get him better! Nan wants our help. Apparently, we're having a Beltane celebration tonight.'

'Oh, I love Beltane!' Martha said. 'Of course, we must celebrate it in secret now.'

'How so?' I asked.

'My mother talks about dancing around the maypole with flowers in her hair, but all that stopped. Oliver Cromwell has forbidden the frivolities of May Day. We are no longer allowed to dance in the streets.'

'He sounds like a right party pooper!'

Martha laughed, then clapped her hand over her mouth and looked around.

'It's OK, Oliver Cromwell isn't hiding in the rose bushes,' I said.

Martha sniggered again. 'The Reformation has made life very dull indeed! You cannot be too sure, though. You never know who's listening. Who is going to go running to the authorities with tales of wrongdoing?'

We worked all day, picking flowers and making garlands for our hair. We made elderflower cordial and lemon drizzle cake and gathered a big pile of wood for the fire. Nan was going up and downstairs to Grandad all day, and I sent up a bunch of sweet peas for her to put in his bedroom with my love. Just as the sun was setting over the hill in the west, Nan came out. She was wearing a long white dress, tied at the waist with a flowery scarf. I passed her a flower crown and she placed it on her head. She looked beautiful. Martha and I placed our flower crowns on each other's heads.

'Did you ring Mam back, Nan?' I asked as she bent down and put a match to the paper in the fire.

'No, Molly, I've not had time. Come on, we need more wood on here.' She got a bunch of sage and threw that on the fire. 'The fire is to cleanse, Molly, to heal. We cast out the darkness and welcome the light!'

I looked up at the Velux windows in the roof, to the attic room where Grandad was lying. I ached that he couldn't be down here with us.

'Have you checked on Grandad recently, Nan?'

'Yes, Molly, not half an hour ago, before I came out. He was sleeping calmly. I am not totally irresponsible, you know!'

'I'm sorry, Nan, I'm just really worried.'

'Ssh! Yes, I know you are, and so am I. But we must have faith, Molly.'

We warmed ourselves by the fire, Nan swigging out of a bottle of homemade elderberry wine, Martha and me with mugs of spicy hot apple juice. As the light faded, bats flittered around in the dusk, their wings beating so fast you could hardly see them, twisting, turning, swooping. I would have been scared of these a month or so ago, but now they just seemed normal, part of this wild world in which I was now living. We watched the fire for ages without saying anything. I know Nan and I were both thinking of Grandad, and I guessed Martha was thinking of her mother. She'd not said very much all day, but that was fine. It wasn't every day you found out your mother was hanged and had to decide whether to stay in 2020, in the time and place you have time-travelled to, or return to the life you knew, in the seventeenth century, hunted and demonised for being different. I thought about this whole fitting-in thing. I had tried so hard, going along with all the beautiful people at school. I had tried to tame my wild hair, tugging at it every day with straighteners. I had tried to lose weight to fit in with the media image of what a girl should look like. But I knew I was different. I was sick of trying to create this false Molly in order to fit in, and I made a promise to myself, there and then, to be proud of who I was and not to try and act out and be something I was not. It was time to get off the stage and be the real Molly McFlynn, with wild hair and chunky thighs who liked to eat cake.

'Go and get that saxophone,' Nan said out of the blue. 'The one that belonged to your mother. It's under your bed.'

'But I don't know how to play it,' I said.

'It doesn't matter, we are going to blow the very breath into Joe's body,' Nan said, reaching into her pocket for her penny whistle and picking up a drum. She was clearly drunk, but I went along with it. I had a feeling I couldn't explain. The hairs on my arms had stood on end. It was as if maybe, just maybe, this might work. Nan gave Martha the penny whistle. 'Here, blow!' she said, and started to bang out a beat on her drum, walking around the fire, chanting and singing.

What a sight we must have been. And what a noise! Nan dancing round the fire in her white robes, banging her drum and shouting, me stood on top of the garden table playing Mam's old saxophone. I made a terrible din but gave it all I could. Martha was laughing so much she could hardly blow a note. Meg joined in too, barking and charging around the garden. It was a good job Nan and Grandad didn't have any neighbours apart from the farm. You certainly couldn't have done this in Heaton! I blew and blew until there was no puff left in me. Nan sang, and chanted, and although it was weird, I joined in too with everything I had. We were just letting rip, sounds, songs, screams, beats from the drum, blasts from the saxophone, toots and screeches from Martha's penny whistle. With every breath I imagined Grandad breathing for himself, his chest rising and falling. He had to live! He had to breathe.

'Would you just listen to that racket,' a voice said, coming though the dark and down the garden path.

'Mam!' I screamed.

I ran towards her, but she held out her arm.

'No hugging, Molly. I know it's hard, but I'm going to keep my distance. I've been up to check on Dad. He was better than I thought he'd be, chuckling with all the noise you lot are making. Now, do you want to give me that saxophone?'

Mam got some antiseptic wipes from her handbag, wiped down the mouthpiece and keys, and took the saxophone from me. She put it to her lips and played. The notes were haunting, rich, and I started to breathe deeper, feeling the music down in my chest. I looked over at Nan. She was holding her hand on her heart, her chin quivering, and tears were streaming down her face.

Then Nan started to sing, and Mam played along, a quiet song, beautiful and as clear as crystal. Martha moved closer to me, and we held hands. It was a clear night; the stars were out, and the half-moon now shone bright. The fire had burned low, with golden embers on the ground.

'I'm so glad you're here,' Nan said. 'Together we make the triune: crone, mother and maiden. We've one final thing to do.'

'What's that?' I asked.

'We are going to jump the Beltane fire, Molly,' Mam said with a grin, looking at Nan. 'I haven't done this for a very long time.'

Mam reached into her bag, gave her hands a quick rub with gel, then grabbed my hand and Nan's too. I grabbed Martha, and we took a running jump, and together leapt into the air and across the fire.

Twenty-Three

The Triune

It was as if we were in slow motion. Despite Nan's dodgy knees and my sore ankle, we cleared the hot embers and landed on the other side, still holding hands. There it was again, that feeling like an electric current was passing through my hands, as if something very powerful was at play. My mother turned to face her mother, and the moonlight shone in the tears that flowed down both women's cheeks.

'I love you,' Nan said in a voice that was hardly more than a whisper.

'And I love you,' Mam said, 'and when this pandemic is over, I'm going to give you the biggest hug I can.'

A light went on in one of the Velux windows in the roof, and a face appeared at the window.

'Grandad!'

Mam, Nan and I rushed inside and up the stairs.

Grandad was sitting on the edge of his bed, his bedside light on. 'That racket was enough to wake the dead!' he said, a weak smile on his face.

Mam and I stood at his bedroom door, but Nan slapped on a mask and rushed in, wrapping her arms around him, his hand stroking the top of her head.

'We did it. We did it,' Nan said though her sobs.

'Oh, you had us worried there, Dad,' Mam said. 'If you didn't pull round tonight, you were coming to hospital with me first thing in the morning.'

'Well, I'm back now,' Grandad said, his voice croaky, and then he started coughing.

'Doesn't sound as if you're out of the woods yet,' Mam said, 'but we'll stand that ambulance down, eh, Mam?'

My nan looked back at Mam and nodded. 'I reckon so.'

'Come on,' Mam said to me, 'we'll leave these two love birds alone. Why don't you introduce me to your friend?'

*

Martha had stayed by the bonfire and had got it roaring again. She was stood the other side of the flames, her body and face lit up with an orange glow. It was hard to make out in the dark, through the flames, but there appeared to be some sort of shimmering form next to her. I looked closer and saw a tall woman with long silver hair. She was dressed from head to toe in silver, the flames reflecting in the sparkles on her clothes. She was fizzing like a firework. And then she was gone.

'Who was that?' I asked Martha.

'Who was who?'

'Ah, nothing, I thought I saw... never mind. It looks like my grandad is going to be alright after all,' I said to Martha.

'I am so pleased for you,' she said.

'Mam, I haven't introduced you to my friend, have I? Mam, this is Martha, and Martha, this is my mam. Martha's from the seventeenth century.'

'Now, Molly, don't be rude. Don't insult someone just because they don't keep up with fashion like you and your friends.'

'Molly has told me a lot about you,' Martha said.

'Not all bad, I hope!' Mam said.

'Oh no, not at all! She tells me you are a nurse and are helping sick people, just like my mother does...' Then Martha went quiet and stared at the flames in the fire.

Mam went back inside, clearing up the plates and glasses as she went.

'Molly,' Martha continued, 'I have decided that I must go back. I am going to find the portal, try to get back to my own time. If my mother is to be executed, then I want to be there. I want her to see me in the crowd, see someone who loves her.'

As she spoke, the same woman I'd seen through the flames came up beside Martha and laid her hand on her shoulder. 'And I will be the one to guide Martha on her journey, just like I helped her the first time.'

'Who are you, and what do you mean?' I asked.

'My name is Freya. I sometimes take human form, other times the shape of a hare. You girls may well have noticed hares crossing your paths, guiding you when you were lost. Well, I have been taking care of you all.

I am a goddess, a witch, some might call me, but I am a protector.'

This had just gone up to a whole new level of weird.

'I've been finding bits of silver all over the place!' I said. 'Bits of fluff, thread and sparkly bits. I've collected them in a box upstairs.'

'I keep seeing silver light, like the day I came through the portal, and again, when I escaped from the lads at the camp, in the storm,' Martha said.

Freya stood up and held an arm out for Martha and, in a voice that sounded like liquid silver, said, 'The time has come for you to return, Martha. Your mother needs you.'

'Molly, will you fetch the Gathering?' Freya asked. 'Martha needs to return it to her time.'

Freya walked down the garden with Martha, and I went inside to get Nan and the Gathering.

Nan came out with the Gathering and her piece of embroidery. She gave them both to Martha. She did not seem to see Freya, and neither did Mam.

'Martha, if you get the chance, will you give your mother this piece of needlework and tell her that we are all with her? We may not be able to be with you in real time, but we will remember your mother on the date of her execution, every year from now on 21 August. We know she has done nothing wrong, and years down the line, she will be remembered as a victim of persecution by the patriarchy. We will shout her story loud and that of the other women with her.'

It was my turn. I did not want to say goodbye to my friend. In the two months that I had known her, she had been more of a friend to me than any of my friends back in town. She had taught me that it was OK to be me, that I didn't need straightened hair or the latest disposable fashion. I didn't need to seek approval from others, bend over backwards for the lads. I could just be me, and that was OK. I knew I would never see her again as we held each other, but I knew I would keep the memory of her mother alive. I would write everything down that she had told me. The stories of women buried in history must be told.

'Hang on a minute!' I said, and raced inside, coming out with my purple Docs.

'You can't walk all the way back to town in those!' I said, pointing to her wooden-soled shoes. Then I took my Pandora ring off and gave it to Martha. 'Here, Martha, I want to give you my ring. It is silver, with an opal, a moonstone. I hope it will always remind you of me, your time here, and bring you good luck.'

'I cannot, it is too precious. You have already given me your shoes!'

'Yes, you can. I insist.'

'Then I insist you have this.' Martha slipped off the crescent moon and tied it around my wrist.

We hugged, neither of us able to speak and both of us with tears in our eyes.

She left wearing my purple Docs, with the Gathering tucked under her arm, walking down the moonlit lane with Freya by her side. As they reached the top of the hill, she turned and waved. Then Martha disappeared over the brow and out of my life.

Meg came and sat at my feet, looking up at me with her big brown eyes. I reached down, stroking her neck as I stood on the lane and watched, half-hoping Martha would change her mind and come back, but she didn't, and that was OK too.

'Come on, Meg, bedtime.' This had been the strangest two months of my life.

Twenty-Four

Leaving

Over the next few days, Grandad continued to get better. It was amazing! It wasn't long before he could sit in a chair in the garden with a blanket wrapped around him. Nan popped out with a spoonful of medicine from time to time, with plates of sandwiches, pots of tea and cake, but was very busy with her own work too, making remedies and delivering them on her bike. Mam sat with Grandad in the garden. They had so much to talk about, so much lost time to make up for. Grandad's smile was back, his laughter lines crinkling around his eyes; he had got his little girl back, and Mam had got her daddy back.

I left them to talk, still busy in the greenhouse and garden, potting up seedlings, planting and weeding. It was a full-time job, but I loved it! I had always loved gardening as a little girl and hadn't realised how much I missed those days, helping Grandad to sow peas and dig up potatoes.

He'd sown the seeds of something in me at a very young age, and now this love of growing was being well watered. I understood now why they grew their own food, how much better it tasted and how much better it was for you. I'd never felt so well! My energy levels were so much better than when I used to eat all that sugar and rubbish. My skin looked great, and I might have chipped nails with garden dirt under them most of the time, but this was how I wanted to be, with my hands in soil, rooted in the earth.

Nan and Grandad had taught me about eating seasonally and not buying food that had been shipped from all around the world, grown under plastic and arriving in the supermarkets wrapped in single-use plastic. I felt an urgency now, that it was time to change, to do my bit to help the climate crisis. For far too long I'd walked around in ignorance, not making the connection that I could do my bit, that if we all consumed a whole lot less, our planet might not be headed for destruction. It wasn't just food either: I thought of all the cheap clothes I bought then threw away, all the products I had used, all those plastic bottles. In just two months I had gone from hating this way of life to wanting to embrace it, live it and shout it from the rooftops.

I was thinking all this as I was watering the tomato plants in the greenhouse, pulling off the little offshoots, as Nan had shown me. I held one up to my nose. It smelt of here, of my grandparents. The sound of a bicycle bell made me look up. It was the vicar. He dinged the bell again and waved, getting off and leaning the bike on the fence.

'Molly! How are you? Recovered from your ordeal, I hope?'

I came out of the greenhouse and went up to the roadside. 'What do you want?' I asked.

'I wanted to speak to you, Molly, say how sorry I was about how the community responded to the homeless person in the woods. I should have taken the good Lord's example when he helped those less fortunate than himself. We think of the parable of the Good Samaritan, of course.'

'You should have helped, Vicar. You didn't.'

'Please, Molly, call me Simon. I wanted to speak to you and your grandmother too.'

'Uh, oh, what's she done now?' I said with a smile.

Simon laughed. 'It's nothing bad. I was given this electric bike. I wondered if your nan would like it. I see her cycling around the village, delivering parcels. Perhaps this would help her get around a bit easier.'

'I'm sure she would! She'd always complaining about her knees!'

'Excellent. I'll leave it here, Molly, and walk back up to the vicarage.'

'I just did what I thought was right,' I said.

'You set an example to us all, Molly, about kindness and generosity of spirit.'

'Like I said, I just did what I thought was right.'

'Well, let's hope whoever it was has found a safe place to live now. I understand they have moved on.'

I hoped with all my heart that Martha was safe, had found kindness when she returned to Newcastle in 1649, but I doubted it. I imagined her visiting the tower where her mother was being held, talking to her through a grate in the floor, the stench rising, her mother slowly losing her mind with the torture she would endure, with only her

223

execution to look forward to. It was a desperate situation. To be honest, I tried not to think of it too much. What could I do? She had made her choice to go back.

'Give my regards to your grandfather, too,' Simon said. 'We've been praying for him, you know.'

'Thank you,' I said. 'I will.'

The vicar walked off down the lane, and I went down to the veggie patch to pick some spinach. I thought I'd make spanakopita for lunch. That's the proper name for spinach pie, and it was now one of my favourites.

*

'You, eating spinach?' Mam said, as I took the spanakopita out of the oven and placed it on the table. 'And all that pastry!'

'Yeah, I eat spinach now.'

'Who'd have thought?'

Nan placed her hand on Mam's, in a gesture that said 'be quiet'.

'It's good food, Mam, not packed full of chemicals. I'm done with diet charts, food plans and the rest. I'm going to eat what I want when I want. I've had it with comparing myself to others, with trying to be something I'm not.'

'Sorry I spoke!' Mam said.

'No, seriously, Mam, I want to be positive about my body. I get that I used to eat rubbish, and I get that that was not good for me. But I'm not interested in weighing myself anymore. I want to be healthy in mind and in body.'

'Let's eat,' Nan said. 'It looks delicious, Molly. I always love this dinner this time of year, so fresh.'

'I put some nettle tops in it too,' I said. 'They're full of iron. I saw it in an Instagram post.'

Mam's face was a picture, but Nan just beamed with pride.

'That's my girl,' Grandad said.

I took a photo of my plate and uploaded it to Instagram. My account which I'd called 'Molly's Garden' was doing well. I had over a thousand followers. This sustainable living stuff, growing your own food and eating seasonally, was really taking off. I guessed Nan and Grandad had been doing it all their lives. But it was great it was becoming more mainstream.

'That was delicious, Molly,' Mam said, having eaten a whopping piece of pie, new potatoes and carrots.

'I'll clear up,' Nan said. 'Why don't you both walk the dog down the lane? It's a beautiful evening.'

'Good idea,' I said, 'if you're sure?'

Grandad had done well, but it looked as if he was ready for bed, and if Nan was happy clearing up, then it would be good to spend some time with Mam, just the two of us. We hadn't had much of a chance to be alone. Mam put on a pair of bright white trainers, and I smiled as I laced up my muddy old walking boots. I'd changed in more ways than one!

The sun was still high in the sky, the evening warm, with a breeze moving the grasses in the hay meadows in gentle waves. The hawthorn blossom was fully out now, and the hedgerows full of wildflowers.

'I've been drawing these,' I said to Mam. 'That pink one is campion, that's speedwell, and this one,' I said, cupping my hand under a cluster of tiny white flowers, 'is

225

sweet cicely. You can use it instead of sugar when you cook rhubarb.'

Mam was laughing.

'What's funny?'

'You are.'

We carried on walking. The wind was blowing the tall grass in the fields like waves on water. A curlew rose hovering over the grass with that bubbling sound that will always remind me of being here.

Mam put her arm around me as we walked. 'Your dad would be proud of you too.'

I stopped walking and turned to look at her. 'You never talk about him – why now?'

'I've been thinking a lot about him lately. There's so much about him I miss. But so much I don't too!'

'I think I understand a bit more now, Mam. He must have been impossible at times!'

'He just refused to grow up! Was always chasing the good times, never taking any responsibility. I felt it was all down to me. I got bitter, resentful and forgot how to have any fun myself.'

'I'm not surprised, Mam, it must have been tough. I'm sorry I was so angry with you.'

It felt good to talk to Mam like this. It was as if she were talking to me as an adult, as a friend and not a silly child. We reached the green bridge and walked onto the middle of it. It had seen some action over these past two months! I looked over to the spot where I'd first seen Martha, the day I lost the plot on the bridge. My heart ached as I thought of her again. I wanted to know so badly that she was alright. But there was no way of knowing. I could only hope. I watched the water, calm now, clear. You could see the bottom, the rocks and weeds in the river. There were fishermen further down, stood in the river in waders, flicking their rods into the water, trying to catch trout and salmon. It had been a very different river in the storm.

It was a very different picture too, up on the bridge: me, Mam and the sun shining on our faces. As I bent over the green railing, watching the river flow, something bright blue flashed along, just above the surface of the water, under the bridge, then on down the river in the direction of town. It was the kingfisher. Was this a sign that everything was going to be OK? Not just for me but for Martha, for Grandad too? I remembered Nan reading the tea leaves, the bird she saw, and Grandad telling me that a kingfisher was a sign of better days to come. I hoped so.

*

I woke the next morning to the sound of sheep and their lambs from the fields that surrounded the house, bleating as they anticipated the arrival of the farmer's quad and their feed. It was so loud! I would miss all this, but it was time to leave. I could have stayed on a bit longer, but I reckoned Mam could do with a bit of help around the flat, and I was ready to go back to town now. I had a mountain of schoolwork to do, too. Now Mam, Nan and Grandad had made their peace I could always come back and visit. The station is just down the lane and there's a direct train from Newcastle to here. Well, you need to plan your day, as there are only three trains a day that stop here.

I got out of bed and opened the curtains, looking out of the window and onto the garden, remembering the first night, when I'd seen Nan picking mugwort by the light of the moon, and the silver light, and the hare that had sat in the garden after she had disappeared. Was that Freya all along, shapeshifting into a hare, or was it was just Nan? Or was it just a plain old brown hare that had chosen to have its baby in Nan's garden? Sometimes you don't have the answer; you can believe what you want to believe. I wanted to believe that Freya was still watching over Martha. I wanted to believe that she was going to be safe and happy.

As I drew the curtains, the sunlight caught the tray of items I'd collected every time I spotted the hare, or rather, Freya: sequins, coins, bits of fluff, thread and a little silver bell. Silver shapes danced on the wall at the top of the curtains, and as I looked up, I saw something I hadn't noticed before. Carved into the old, wooden lintel, which was full of woodworm holes, was a tiny hare. Could it be? I stretched up and ran my finger in the grooves. A definite hare. Someone had carved a hare in my room. I grabbed the stone Martha gave me on my birthday, the one with the painted hare. It was on my bedside table. I had held it before I went to sleep every night since she left, thinking of her. I held it up next to the carved hare. It was the same design. Martha must have come back.

Hadn't Grandad said these were farm worker's cottages and dated back to the 1500s? Could it be that Martha came back and got work on the farm? Oh, I hoped so! I rushed downstairs to where Nan was sat, making notes in her version of the Gathering.

'Nan! Nan! There's a hare on the lintel. Come and see!'

But Nan just smiled. 'I know, darling,' she said. 'It's been there a very long time.'

'Do you think Martha came back? Did she actually live here?'

'Who knows, Molly.' Nan closed the brown leather cover on her book and ran her fingers over the crescent moon on the cover. 'She found her way here once, so who's to say she didn't do it again? It's a nice thought. Let's hold on to that, shall we?'

It was time to go. Grandad was sat on the sofa, and I sat down next to him. I could see he was struggling to speak, not just because of his cough but because he was all choked up. I was too. I just gave him a big hug, and he patted my back.

'Come back soon, duck,' he said. 'Thanks for all you've done.'

'I'll be back as soon as I can, Grandad. You're going to need my help in that garden of yours, and I want you to teach me all about growing food!'

Nan and I stood on the step while Mam put the bags in the car, our arms around each other.

'Goodbye, my precious, you take care now.'

'See you soon, Nan. I love you.'

A wood pigeon called from the trees opposite.

Epilogue

The Town Moor

There is a single oak tree that stands alone on the Town Moor. Dom was already there, his long hair flying in the wind that was whipping over the exposed ground. I could see Esmée and Jess walking along the path towards us. They were laughing at something, the sound of their voices being carried in the wind as they got closer.

I had made a promise to Martha that I'd remember her and her mother on 21 August every year on the anniversary of her hanging and had asked Dom, Jess and Esmée to meet me.

'What are we doing here?' Jess said. 'It's bliddy freezing.'

They were both wearing matching black and white striped crop tops and trackie bottoms, their bellybutton piercings twinkling in the sun over their flat, tanned stomachs which were prickled with goosebumps from the cold.

'See you've dressed for the weather!' I laughed.

They both looked me up and down. I was wearing the jumper Nan had given me. It had got loads of compliments at the community allotment. I guess sometimes you need to find your tribe, but to be honest, I was learning not to care what people thought anymore. I wore what I felt comfortable in.

'I've come to remember a friend,' I said, 'and to honour the women murdered here for being witches.'

'Witches!' cackled Jess, making her hands into claws.

'Spooky!' Esmée said.

'No, barbaric,' I said. 'Did you know, hundreds of women were brutally murdered for just being different? This is the place where, in 1650, sixteen people were hanged.'

Jess and Esmée looked at each other and made that 'she's such a weirdo' face, that I was getting used to and no longer really minded.

'Molly, how come you've got so heavy on us?'

'It's a long story, but could we just be quiet for a minute?'

I bent and placed the stone hare at the foot of the tree, with a bunch of flowers I'd picked in Heaton Park on the way over. Dom reached for my hand, and despite the odd snigger, Esmée and Jess were respectfully quiet too. I closed my eyes, listened to the sound of traffic on the city ring road and thought of Martha, stood in the crowd of folk jeering, shouting and watching while her mother was taken in nothing more than a dirty shift from the prison to this spot on the moor. The crowds would have been here for entertainment and for justice, to see the witches hanged. Did Martha meet her mother's eye as she was led to the rope? What did she feel as her mother's neck snapped? Did Martha then turn and flee once more, back along the river? Did a silver light guide her? Did she walk by the light of the full moon, back to a new life, free from those who'd persecuted her for being different?

Tears were falling down my face, and when I opened my eyes, Dom was crying too. For once, Jess didn't have anything to say.

'Thank you for coming,' I said, and bent to pick up the stone hare. I wasn't going to leave it there for anyone to pinch.

'We'll be off then. Are you coming down into town?' Jess asked. 'We're going to Maccy D's for milkshakes, then hitting the sales.'

'No, you're alright,' I said. 'I don't need anything new.'

'Since when did needing anything new come into shopping?' Esmée asked.

'You do know, the amount of waste clothing we chuck away every year would fill Wembley Stadium to the brim?'

'Nah, lost on me, Molly,' Jess said. 'Never been to Wembley. Now, if you'd have said St James' Park… You've gone all green on us, haven't you?'

'Yeah, guess so. I just think we need to look after the planet a whole lot better, and besides, I've got things to do,' I said, a smile growing on my face.

'Oh, yeah?' Dom said with a grin. 'Come on, spill the beans, Molly. Who are you meeting?'

'If you must know, I'm meeting a friend at the community allotment.'

'A lad?' Jess asked.

232

'Yes, he's a boy and he's just a friend,' I said. 'Look, thanks for coming, say hi to everyone else, but I've got to go.'

We went our separate ways and I set off to walk to Ouseburn and the community allotment where I had met Jez, who was just a friend, but I was hoping it might grow into something more. He was two years older than me, was in the sixth form, had long hair he was growing into dreadlocks, and was into dub and reggae. We'd hung out together a few times, just talking, just listening to music, and unlike the other guys at school, like Gareth Swindle, he hadn't tried it on.

As I walked, I looked up and across to town and the Civic Centre building in the distance. The sun caught the windows and a silver light winked back.

Acknowledgments

I have wanted to write a book and see it on the shelves of a book shop ever since I was a small girl and would sew pages together to make my own books, illustrating them with coloured pencils. Now my dream has come true. I am a published author. Thank to all of you who have bought this book and read it.

I would like to thank the team at the Book Guild for reading my submission, giving Molly McFlynn a home, and telling me they found my work unique and exciting. Thank you for holding the hand of this fledgling author and answering a myriad of questions. Thank you to the marketing team for making sure my book is seen far and wide.

Ann Coburn who sparked my imagination in the Writing for Children and Young Adults module at Newcastle University deserves a special mention. Under her tutelage and then mentorship, she helped me craft my work and make Molly into the special character that she is. Thank you, Ann for believing in Molly and me, for your expert knowledge, patience and enthusiasm and for writing such a beautiful endorsement.

Thanks to Lars Iyer who tutored me as this work was

entered in my final portfolio at Newcastle University, for your encouragement and insistence on narrative action.

Tracy Burdon, a fellow student on my MA deserves a special mention as she played a large part in holding my hand as I wrote, encouraging me when self-doubt crept in and then afterwards in the editing process. Tracy, thank you for reading every word, for your proofreading and editing skills but above all for your friendship and encouragement.

Thank you to my dear daughter Hannah, who also has given shed loads of encouragement and believed that her mum would one day be a published writer. Her proof reading skills were also much appreciated. As a bookseller of Waterstones, I can't wait until she sells the first copy of my book to a customer and tells them, 'my mum wrote that'. Indeed, thank you to all my family for your support and enthusiasm.

Thanks to the staff at Cogito Books in Hexham, and to Hilary, for your encouragement and advice about the publishing and book selling industries.

Thank you to Caren Thompson for allowing me to include the Silver Spoon Collective project in the story.

Thanks to Louise Hick for producing the beautiful artwork from which the inspiration for the cover design came. It was so good to chat about ecofeminism around the log fire in your studio.

Thank you to my followers and supporters on social media. You are all fantastic! Those of you who were Woolly Pedlar followers but stayed loyal and now follow my writing, thank you. Now this book is out in the world, thank you for waiting patiently. I hope you enjoy reading it.

The biggest thank you, which I've left until the end goes to my husband Tim. Thank you for standing by me for over half a century, but more specifically in the new chapters I carve for myself. Thank you for getting over the shock relatively quickly when I announced I was giving up The Woolly Pedlar and going to university to do my MA in Creative Writing. Thank you for supporting me, and for encouraging me to keep going when I wanted to give up. Thank you for believing in me. I love you.

Author's Note

This novel was part inspired by the Newcastle witch trails which began in 1649 and ended when fifteen (or sixteen – the records are unclear) women and one man were hung by the neck on the Town Moor, Newcastle in 1650. Ann Watson was one of those accused of being a 'wych'. We do not know anything else about her. We do know that a witchfinder was employed from Scotland to search out those suspected of witchcraft were rounded up from the streets of Newcastle and in 1649 Ann Watson was flung in the dungeons to await trial and sentencing.

As part of the Medicine Spoon Memorial Project, I was invited to embroider a small piece of fabric by artist Caren Thompson who had collected the names of the hundreds of women brutally murdered on accusations of witchcraft during the time known as the 'burning times'. I asked if any of the names of those hanged in Newcastle were available, and I got Ann Watson.

Ann Watson is the only character in the story based on fact, apart from a brief mention of Boris Johnson who announced the first lockdown. All other characters are fictitious.

I wanted to write a book that bears witness to the women whose stories are not known, who are unseen, but dared to be different. The othering of women and girls is not something new, and in my creation of Molly McFlynn I wanted to show a girl who learns that it is ok to be different, that we do not have to create a false self in order to fit in.

In this first book, Molly is turned on to a way of living that is gentle and in tune with the seasons as Mother Nature intended. In future Molly McFlynn adventures, Molly will meet other women from history, hear their stories and in doing so grow in her understanding of herself as she comes of age whilst taking on an environmental issue pertinent to the times we are in now.

I began writing this novel during my MA in Creative Writing at Newcastle University, tutored by Ann Coburn in the module 'Writing for Children and Young Adults' in 2020. It wasn't long before lockdown was announced, and all teaching went online. I have spent the last couple of years working with Ann as a writing mentor to bring this first book in the Molly McFlynn series to you.

I hope that young people struggling with their identity, or finding their place in the world will identify with Molly as she finds hers. As for older readers, I hope you will find plenty to identify with: feeling like an outsider can be something we grapple with all our lives.

I do hope you enjoy the read and would love to have your feedback. If you have time to leave a review on Amazon or Good Reads that would be amazing, and you can find me on Sue Reed Writes across most social media channels.

About the Author

Sue Reed lives in rural Northumberland where a love of nature informs her work. She had a career in teaching, writing curricula and sensory drama for children with severe learning difficulties, then ran her own business upcycling waste wool knitwear as The Woolly Pedlar. In 2019 she studied for her MA in Creative Writing at Newcastle University. She writes about sustainable living at The Bridge Cottage Way. *The Rewilding of Molly McFlynn* is her debut novel.